THE BUTCHER'S DAUGHTER

A NOVEL OF ABUSE AND REDEMPTION

BEATE DAYEM STAMNESS

Cover art by Erika Rothfuss König

Cover design by Charles Kealey

 Created with Vellum

ACKNOWLEDGMENTS

THANK YOU

My dearest family, for reading and critiquing yet another book of mine. Jesse, Jim, Miette, Mike and Jenny, you were a most enthusiastic cheering section. And Lin, truly an editor par excellence.

Joyce Higgins, you found the little inconsistencies everybody else missed. I am very grateful for you and your suggestions!

Thanks to my early readers Kathy Ferrando, Bob Breen and Kelly McClelland. I appreciated every crumb of praise or valuable criticism.

Dani Burlison, teacher and writer, without your constant encouragement, I might have never written anything at all.

CONTENTS

1

A KIDNAPPING

Father's sharp knife slices through piles of meat, blood dripping over his filthy apron, the hair on his pale hands and arms freckled in ghoulish red dew. Mother clomps about in heavy boots waving a cleaver in her hand. The sounds and sights seep into my dream, then startle me awake as I desperately try to hold on to the memories of who I am and who they were, the man and the woman that used to be my parents.

She wore blue, and the blue was torn along her shoulder, stained with the blood that gushed from her head and reddened her blonde hair into a stringy mess. He was dark; I liked how he smelled. There were others, my brothers most likely, I can't see them now, but they were running. My sister, too, was running. She was maybe called Uscha. I can't be sure. Her face is gone. All their faces are gone. And that's the last time I saw them, the people I believe to be my family. They live on as shadows, hidden away and brought to life only in the dark of night so the others won't know.

I am now a butcher's daughter, call them Mother and Father. But I am holding on to the dreams, keep them alive or I might get lost in my new world of animals being led to slaughter, and the meats we eat that taste of their screams.

"My poor little girl, how you must have suffered," she repeated over and over. "My poor little girl, left in a filthy ditch, anybody could have taken you. You might have died." She deeply sighs. "How lucky I found you."

I was in shock, gripped by fear, suffocating from the screams that wouldn't come out. Wanted my Mother, wanted her face and feel her arms around me, still heard her frantic shrieks from far away. I was NOT left in a ditch. Mother put me down because of the blood, and when she picked me up again it was HER, who I call Mother now, who ran away with me, a blanket thrown over my head. I wanted to kick her out of my life, screamed till it hurt, but she held me with the force of steel against her breasts, a struggling little animal caged inside the blanket. She ran for a long time, slowly leaving behind the chaos of sounds and people running, whole cities of people running and pounding the ground with their feet. She never let go of her deadly grip. Then I slept.

I awoke to an eerie quiet. A disturbing quiet, not the way it should sound and feel. The harsh wind in the trees was tearing off its leaves in sudden gusts, then held its breath for the next attack. A large black bird squawked by, settled in the tree above, neither chirping nor singing but with the scary sound of one that circles for its next meal. Already, the sound of pounding footsteps was a faint memory. Then she ran again, and I struggled, and then I slept some more and had no struggle left and no voice when I woke up. And when the blanket opened onto a stranger's face far from my family, from their faces and footsteps, something died inside of me from fear and a bottomless grief.

"What's your name?" She asked in a voice that was wrong and raspy. I could not answer and didn't know how much time had passed. She tried to feed me, but I could not eat.

"What's your name?" She asked again and again. Then she tried feeding me again and I took a bite because of my hunger.

"Good girl," she said. "And now what is your name?"

"Monika," I answered, in a whisper of hope. Please let me be Monika.

"You need a proper name," she mumbled, "then you can be my very own little girl."

And from then on, I was Klara Fleischer.

Many years have gone by since. I am eight years old now and live on the very edge of a small town in Germany, not too far from the border with the East. The house is small with the main entry door leading into the butcher store. It is made of glass. Another small wooden door to its left leads into our kitchen. Store and kitchen are connected on the inside. Behind the kitchen is a forbidden room which I have never entered. It's were they sleep. Then there is an outhouse in the backyard beyond our two large, chained and growling Rottweilers. They give me a fright each time I walk by to use it.

Behind the store is a dark, dank area where Father kills the animals before hanging them on large hooks. They attract flies. It is a dirty, smelly place and it spooks me to think of all the butchered animals that used to live, then died and are no more.

But I need to be grateful they tell me. And when Father towers over me in his large frame and scares me out of my wits with his rat's eyes then I am truly grateful to still be alive. During the war, he only came home on weekends. Now he is here all the time, the mean, dirty son of a bitch. Truly, that's how we talk in this house, and I barely know what's good or bad, right or wrong.

A narrow wooden staircase leads from the kitchen to my small room under the roof. A little window looks down into the large backyard. Rusty engines, tools and parts of broken machines seem to grow out of the dirt. There is no green. I am sitting on my bed with its metal frame. My bedding has been boiled and mended within a breath of its life. I used to wet it and Father spanked me hard. Giving me pain causes him the only pleasure he knows. It makes his eyes fill with a crazy glint and his body puffs up for the punches.

Next to my bed is a wooden stand with a pretty bowl and matching water pitcher painted with daisies. In the morning, the sun shines onto the little flowers and into the room, making dust swirls in the sun-lit air. Those tiny specks of dust dance with each other like my brothers and sisters, thousands of them. They dance, then they leave, and I am alone. Always alone.

I would love to have a cat to snuggle with and to tell her my dreams, tell her who I used to be so that I won't forget and fade away; but cats make me sneeze and the rats outside need them more.

Our house is cold even in summer. It's a cold born of fear. His screams give me shivers. His words hurt and his face frightens me. He and Mother are in the store getting ready for the day, cutting and slicing meat, rattling the cash register, counting coins, and on my way to the little shit encrusted outhouse I stick in my head and whisper 'good morning.' Mother hands me a slice of tongue and a bit of liverwurst. I stuff both in my mouth and thank her.

"Go eat your bread, drink your milk and get going. Hurry. We need you back," she yells. They always need me and tell me the same day after day, 'You'll be a butcher's wife soon. It's hard work, get used to it.'

Why do I need to be a butcher's wife, I wonder? Is that all there is? I don't know what else there could be, I just know there must be something for me to make a difference besides meat. Dead meat.

"Stop dreaming, get your ass out of here," he growls.

I take the rusty green bike and pedal along, a bit wobbly since the seat is too high for me to sit on. It used to be Father's before his ass got too fat.

On a cloudy late summer's day, still warm without any of winter's cold breath, I see the neighbor girl on her way to school. She is one grade above me. I know her name, Monika, because her Mother called her once to come in for dinner, and I was glad. It reminded me of my own real name, Monika, before they turned me into Klara. Without her, I might have lost the little there was left of me. She doesn't know how grateful I am since we cannot play together. Mother and Father don't let me talk to her who has my name, nor to anybody else. They do not give reasons nor answers to any of my questions. And so I learned to be alone, not say much and live in my two worlds, the dream world of shadows that run away, of a bloodied blue dress and snuggles from her who wears it, and the other world, the real world of meat cleavers and screams.

At school, I hide in the back, my face down like Father's, my hair falling over it. I never say a word to anybody. I think I would like to but don't. It is safer to stay invisible. I also worry what might come out of my mouth when I open it. Seems that my kind of words piss everybody off. But I listen, observe and learn. Only the easiest of questions come my way. I answer them quietly, eyes down. Nobody knows I have all the answers; it's best that way. Boisterous kids get whipped, and I had enough of that at home. But no more. Now I bend myself any which way needed to please them.

"Yes, Mother. Yes, Father. Of course, and I am grateful." Life is an obstacle course that needs smooth running for my own good.

From a window in the schoolyard I see a piano inside the school's music room. Nobody ever plays it. My fingers get itchy by the sight of it, and every day the urge to touch this old dusty piece of wood gets stronger as if my life depended on the music hidden beneath its cover. Today during recess, where nobody will miss me, I sneak inside to touch it, let my hands run over the smooth curve of its lid. Then I lift it slightly for just one sound, then a few more. Don't know what's come over me. The cover wants lifting all the way up, and all ten fingers play at once, racing over those keys on their own, driven by an unknown force. The sound causes a stir inside of me, a recognition of some sort. Someone used to play this instrument with magic fingers that could make it sing and my heart would skip along with it. I was sitting on her lap.

Her. It was a woman. I see the shape of her hands, hard-working and capable hands.

The door screeches open and startles me. A new lady teacher is coming in.

"Aren't you supposed to be outside?" she asks, her face a smile like a slice of apple, and somehow, I trust her. It is a new feeling.

"I wanted to hear what it sounds like," I say, "sorry." I try to run away around her, but she catches me by my arm. "Not so fast. May I play something for you, would you like that?"

Filled with a strange hope I nod my head.

She sits down, asks me to sit next to her, then plays the most beautiful music. Deep sobs shake my body from an emotion that was locked inside and is finding its way out; I don't know why. She looks at me, a bit distressed.

"Are you all right, little one?"

"I don't know. I don't know at all." Tears are streaming down my cheeks as I get up and run away.

When school is over, I go back home, quickly and quietly.

"I am home," I call. They close the store for the midday meal, and we sit down together and eat. Always meat and potatoes, even on Fridays when Catholics are not supposed to eat meat is what I've learned at school. If they eat it, they'll go to hell. I don't tell them about it and am waiting for them to soon go to hell, the bitch and the asshole.

"What did you learn?" he wants to know every day in a monotonous voice, his only emotion besides screaming.

"Nothing," I answer every day. And somehow, he seems pleased about it, every day.

2

THE AWAKENING

The music room becomes my sanctuary, my greenhouse. Light streams in through the leaves of a tall tree, and sparrows and finches add their own music to ours. Frau Rittenmaier, the new music teacher, joins me every day at recess, shows me a few things and then lets me try them. She smiles a lot, says 'nicely done,' and within the shortest of times I learn how to play the piano. Easy pieces at first, but I hunger for more, learn the rhythms, the notes and scales and practice on the virtual piano that waits for me like a friend in the tiny corner of my room. I imagine its wooden legs carved into intricate patterns. I conjure up its keys, feel my fingers push them down, and I learn. Learn from wanting to learn. It's been inside of me all along, bottled up. Now, key by magic key, it comes alive. The tiniest expansions of body and soul are taking root. There is a hope in this. A hope that one day my whole truth will emerge. I'll be a butterfly then, reborn in bright colors like those Frau Rittenmaier wears.

. . .

She peers into my eyes like nobody ever did; with admiration.

"Girl," she says, with her voice high and clear as a church bell, "you have talent, real talent." She softly squeezes my shoulder, and a piece of me melts. I feel my own blossoming. It rushes through me like a rain in the desert that brings to life wonders of nature overnight.

At home that day, when he asks me what I learned, I ask "Father, may I have a piano, please?"

He just butchered an animal. Now he scratches his yellow hair with unwashed hands into a bloody mess. He joins us at the table, his face red with anger, his nose purple from the drink, his huge ass nearly breaking the chair. I bend myself into as small a shape as I can.

"I am sorry, Father. I am grateful for your food and for the clothes and for my room. I don't deserve it." This is my litany whenever I am frightened.

"A piano. Goddamn you! We are working our hands bloody for you stinking pile of shit!" And his ugly lips scrunch out, those ugly, spongey lips that hunger for a kill. It takes all my courage to respond and not melt into nothing.

"Sorry Father, I will never mention it again, never!" I do not look into his eyes. It would provoke him, and he'd pounce on me like an animal.

He puts down his fork and knife, rests his filthy hands on the table. They are small and doughy with stubby fingers. Mother is scared. She folds herself into a little bird and timidly stretches out her right hand and puts it on his, a rare gesture and never for love but from fear.

"Father," she says. That's what they call each other, Father and Mother. "It might keep her around the house more easily as she gets older."

"Damn you both," he shouts, his eyes red around the rim and bulging like a frog's, "fucking bitches," and he gets off his chair, balls his hands into tight fists till the knuckles stand out high and white. Then he leaves for the store.

He won't be eating with us now, open mouthed and slurping, drooling and burping. Often, he lifts one of his nasty blubbery buttocks to let go of foul air. Sometimes he farts so bad Mother says he stinks like a three days old corpse left in the sun. He doesn't mind but rather seems to be proud of being praised for something.

I am glad he didn't hit us. Mother quietly unfolds her little self, takes a deep breath and fluffs herself up again. Then the two of us eat in silence. In our house words ring hollow and are worthless.

Upstairs in my room I start to think. That's what growing up means, thinking about things, thinking so hard it hurts. Mother and Father keep me in an empty world stuffed with loneliness and fear. Why did she steal me? There must have been a reason other than to be a butcher's wife. And why do they always wear their bloody aprons except on Sundays. 'For church,' they say but never go. I feel a new courage grow inside of me because of the piano.

Of course, Father does not allow a piano. He doesn't say, it's implied by not getting one. But the school lets me practice during recess and Frau Rittenmaier keeps helping me. When we sit on the bench, I squeeze close to her to feel the beating of her heart, and my fingers keep up with her pulse and fly over the keys with a new lightness and freedom. She is short but she looks tall to me. I like the way her brown hair falls over her small shoulders, a bit unruly, love her smooth skin and big brown eyes, her luscious lips that roll into a plum when she thinks or pouts. I never tasted a plum. Mother doesn't buy fruit and only rarely a cabbage, the green kind. One day, I would like to taste the red kind. I have a feeling that once, a long time ago, I might have liked red cabbage.

Without love and hugs in my life I forgot I had a body. I stare at my toes, my fingers, and all the rest of me, astonished to own it, and my mind expands into something new and beyond. I look up now instead of down and feel taller. Teachers start to smile and encourage me, and there comes the day when I raise my hand for the first time, halfway up in a fist, but the teacher notices. And when I answer his difficult question when no one else had the answer, I glow from pride. I conquered my fear. I was not born to be shy. The next time, I will raise my whole arm way up is what I plan to do.

At home, I say nothing about my piano playing or anything else.

"How was school? What did you learn?"

"Nothing." And he is glad.

3

LIFE IS A BAG OF NOTHING

I turned nine the other day and do even more thinking than ever before. There is nothing else for me to do but think and play the piano. I think about thinking itself. Do I know enough to think properly? I am filled with questions in search of their answers, at times so badly that I nearly burst from lack of knowledge.

The other kids at school look down on me, turn around and whisper behind my back, their noses turned up, but more and more it's mixed with curiosity and a bit of respect. Poor things don't know what to think. I don't mind. I am busy finding new places in my mind and, with a bit more courage, new places in town, like around the corner where I have never been.

It is a dangerous thing to do. Father and Mother know the minute I leave and the minute I need to be back. Father is so private he never even goes to town except once a week in the dark of night, when the moon is gone, and bad things happen. You'll never see him walk around outside. When customers come in the store, he pulls his hat over his eyes and slithers into the back like a snake, a very obese snake. Mother goes out mainly to buy potatoes at a small corner store close by. Once, the grocer gave me an apple. I didn't know what to do, didn't thank him, and I never got another one. Outside, she let me have a bite, then ripped it from me and threw it away, afraid Father might see. She never stops to chat, nor does she ever make eye contact or let her eyes linger over pretty things like a kitten, or the glow of golden and fiery red autumn leaves. A few times a year she takes a bus to the neighboring town to buy items like shoes or buttons. She does not go into the center of our town.

"Go help your Mother cut the meat," he barks in anger when he watches me bent over my homework, worried I might get too smart. I think he is dumb, very dumb and dangerous, and with his bloody meat cleaver in his hand he scares me as much as our chained-up Rottweilers.

"Your knives are too sharp they scare me" I lie, but it's also true.

"Dumb shit." But he doesn't hit me.

Father and Mother used to hit me when I insisted on being Monika and not Klara. They hit me hard when I said they did not find me but snatched me from nice parents, and they hurt me when I refused to be three years old when I knew to be four. I'd hold up five fingers and put down the middle one, the way I had been taught. That's how old I was. Didn't want them to take that away from me, too.

"You are three years old because you are too small to be four," she would yell while putting cigarette burns on my back. And he would gleefully use his tools to cut and hurt me, sharp metal tools in painful shapes. I'd close my eyes and imagined biting off her head. Father, I tied him up and fed him to the rats. How could I let my teeth sink into his disgusting flesh?

When I was a good girl, quiet and invisible, she would give me an extra slice of liverwurst and sing me a good night song with her low, raspy voice. That is, when he was not around. Maybe a long time ago her face was pretty and soft, before she uglied it by what she has become. A hard woman all around, sharp as a butcher's knife with no flesh for tenderness and the beady eyes of a raven. At times, they get an eerie glow in this frigid face of hers and they never look in my eyes but rather to the walls, wishing me away. It's the nose that sticks out, elegant and straight down as does her thick black hair.

At rare times, she puts an arm around me in the shop.

"Klara, won't you help this lady, please?"

I flinch and pull away from her fake love, want to punch her in the face but smile instead knowing that it's not a lack of courage any longer but a certain cleverness that makes me behave.

It was a quiet childhood like I imagine death would be. I made up games with imagined friends and animals. We were nice to each other. Countless hours and days were filled with dreams of what there was. Slowly, shapes changed or disappeared. But I held on to the shadows, the running legs, to the blue shoulder with red blood, and to my age and name, - I AM MONIKA, and one year older than they say, - while I sat in my room, endlessly twirling my hair and sucking it. The twirling helped me keep the shadows alive. When I twirled, I was the keeper of the dream. And in my dreams, I was loved.

. . .

One morning, the neighbor's girl left for her first day of school. A sponge dangled out of her backpack for cleaning her blackboard. I got distraught.

"Please, I want to go to school too, please let me go!"

"You have to be six." 'I AM six years old,' I wanted to yell in despair, but knew better. Instead I begged her to get me books to read, and surprisingly, she got me two books about animals. Not the ones for butchering but exotic ones like tigers and elephants, scorpions and poisonous snakes. Nice books with much writing and colorful pictures. I thanked her profusely to maybe get more books. I didn't but was grateful by what she did.

"Keep them in your room. Don't ever let Father see." She is scared, the bitch.

Those two books taught me how to read and write. Mother showed me the sound of letters, grudgingly and painfully slow, and I practiced them on the dust on the dark wooden floor of my room.

The only conversation I ever tried to have with her during those early years was about God.

"Mother, who does God's hair?"

"Don't talk stupid!"

"But I've seen pictures and his hair does not always look the same."

"Shut up." Then she added "go ask God."

"Is he Catholic?" She mumbled something while walking away.

A year later, when I finally did go to school, there was a girl whose name I forgot. She talked about her Mutti and Vati.

"That's what my Father and Mother were called," I said, "you reminded me of their names, Mutti and Vati."

She almost walked away thinking I was dumb witted but stopped and turned her head around. "Where I come from, we say Mutti and Vati instead of Father and Mother. Those are not proper names."

I never forgot those two words again. It's easier to dream when you can whisper 'Mutti and Vati,' such tender sounds. And one of them played the piano. I am sure she was my real Mother.

I wonder about her, my real Mother, the one who loved me. Is she still alive? Would she still love me? And I wonder about my fake Mother who does not love me. I am getting curious about her. Where does her meanness come from? She must have a reason. I'd like to find out. Father would have to be gone, of course. About once a week he goes out late at night to see friends, he says. We have never met those friends, and nobody ever comes to our house. He comes back very drunk and it's best to stay away, even more so than usual.

The next time he is out Mother is in the kitchen sewing. She sews my clothes out of her own used ones. They are not bad, just mean looking because they look like her with her body smell clinging to the fabric. I writhe with disgust when she pulls them over my head. Why can't she sew me clothes like other kids wear? With lace over the breast and an apron tight around the waist. I would love to wear one of those. Instead I thank her for every morsel thrown my way.

"You are too generous," I say and other unfelt words of thanks, lies really. I sit down across from her. Maybe she will look at me today? She doesn't.

. . .

"Mother, what did you do when you were little? Can you tell me about your parents? About my grandparents?" I add, to make her feel good, like I was the daughter she wanted.

She seems flustered, the old bird. I ruffled her feathers. She takes a big breath and pulls herself together.

"I don't know. I guess I was like you always wanting things."

"Did your parents give you things?"

"What are you asking those Goddamn questions for?"

"When I have kids one day, I want to tell them about my Mother and Father and grandparents when they ask. Like I can tell them that you were butchers."

"I wasn't always a butcher."

"Did you want to be one?"

"Hell, no. I couldn't kill a fly. I would have liked to be a seamstress."

"You make me nice clothes," I say, and she smiles. It's the longest and best conversation we ever had, and I don't want it to end. She is ripping a large seam.

"What else would you have liked to do?" Her hands stop ripping and her eyes focus inward. There is something she wants to say, I feel it, but she can't. Instead, her body stars to rock back and force over and over again.

"Did you like music?" I prompt her.

"I took piano lessons." It's barely a whisper.

"And...?"

"Couldn't push the keys hard enough, that's how timid and shy I was. Loud sounds frightened me." She stops rocking, puts down the fabric, gazes at her hands and fingers, heaving a hard sigh. "I've always been weak in every which way."

I should have stopped asking questions, I knew better, I really did. Instead I ask about Father and how they met. She jumps up as if stung by a bee up her butt.

"Leave him out of it, hear me? Don't ever tell him we talk about anything!"

That night I dream about her and wake up with tender thoughts. It's alarming and disturbing. There is nothing tender about her! Mean old goat.

4

A WOMAN OF PASSION, A MAN WITH A SECRET

Morning stress floats up the stairs thick as black smoke. It suffocates and kills any living things and I can't ever get used to their screams. If ever there was any happiness in this house, I imagine it buried in the dirty walls and deep below the ground. I dress, go down, stay out of their toxic way and quietly do my chores with neither a frown nor a smile. Either one might cause trouble. I peel potatoes for the midday meal, eat a piece of liverwurst, drink a cup of coffee, rinse all three of our stained cups in the kitchen sink and hurry to get to school. Learning and playing the piano is my only hope for a better life.

The other kids are getting friendlier. They smile, say 'good morning Klara' and 'tschüss' upon leaving, and when they giggle behind my back, I don't mind adding humor to their lives. At least I am not invisible. But with that reality, a restlessness is growing in me. I feel stifled, chained to my life like our dogs, unloved and unwanted, and life will pass me by. I must take charge of it myself, jump in with both feet. Nobody else will do it for me. During recess, I ask Frau Rittenmaier if she has ANY books for me to read, anything at all, but mostly about the world.

"Klara, why don't you use your library card?" I don't know what that is.

"Do you know where the library is?" I don't know what that is.

"It's right next to city hall, the pretty blue cottage on the left.

"I don't know the town."

Her eyes bore into mine. "What is going on in your life, Klara? Do you need my help?"

"Please, just bring me books if you can, and no, you can't help. Don't even try to help! Please don't help!" And I run away, whispering 'it might hurt.'

The next day at recess she has a surprise for me besides several books.

"You deserve a way better teacher for the piano than I am, and I found a lady who will help you once a week for free, here at school. And Klara, if you ever need me, day or night, come to me, we live right around the corner, my husband and I. Let me show you."

She points to the little white house across the street surrounded by flowers in the ground, on windowsills, and hanging in baskets. She holds me around the waist, and I don't ever want to move. Her touch nearly hurts from pleasure like playing the piano but different. She touches my heart while the piano feeds my soul. Maybe that's the difference between the two words.

"Thank you. Twice a day I pass by and admire it. You look alike, you and your house!"

"Is that a compliment? Me and my old creaky house?"

"You and your house are peaceful and inviting. And beautiful to look at."

"Oh, Klara, you are so sweet." And she gives me an extra squeeze before I run back to class with an ear to ear smile on my face.

Two days later Frau Graf enters the music room and starts a new era the moment she walks in with wide swinging hips. She owns me, owns the room and my whole world. I am grateful to breathe the same air as this sturdy, bossy woman, the opposite of Frau Rittenmaier. Without a word, she walks to the piano, calls me over with her finger and lowers herself onto the bench, using most of it for her butt while I, a bit shy, sink deeply into her hips, almost drowning in their softness. Next she plays a piece of music for an introduction. Her fingers, short, strong and quick as a weasel, wash over the keys with a fury and a brilliance that render me breathless and speechless: those are the hands and fingers from my shadow dreams! Hands that are useful rather than elegant. Goosebumps crawl over my insides and a dizziness from strong vibrations make me nearly faint! She turns her head.

"Are you all right?"

"Feelings have vibrations. I didn't know that." And I let go of my hand that was digging into her with all my might. She might get a black and blue mark!

"We will play such pieces together in no time, you and I. Let's start by having you sit on my coat. You are too low!" She folds her soft woolen coat until I sit high enough. Then she tells me how to hold my arms and use the strength of my gut.

"Grab the keys from the middle, no need to look at your fingers. You can feel them inside the keys."

Her passion is contagious, her strength seeps into me and I

grab those keys without looking, push hard, feel the sound and hear it.

"Wrong," she yells.

"I know," I yell back just as loud, fascinated by my own voice. It is a powerful voice. Where has it been all these years? I can be heard if I want to be.

"If you don't know how to play a piece, sing it. Trust your singing, it will tell you how it wants to be played and when to breathe. Breathe, my girl, breathe from deep down and relax your arms and shoulders. How can your fingers fly if your body is tense?"

And with her green penetrating eyes and bright red curls she makes me do it, and I like when she puts her arms around me when we are done, the way a mother hen does with her chicks, and she says 'good bye, my girl, till next time, and grab those keys with love.' Her bright red lipstick against her white oval freckle face, green earrings that dangle, and the smells of a sweet foreign substance carry me off my feet and I wish every day were next Wednesday.

For the past few days I've taken tiny detours on my way home to explore the town where I live. Then I pedal home so fast they won't notice my stolen minutes. Soon I will be ten years old and need to expand my tiny sliver of a world. We live in a small but pretty town. Of course, it's the only town I have ever seen. It got ignored during the war for its lack of importance and all its buildings are standing in their old glory. It has what looks like the center of town, a marketplace with stores built around it and bustling with people. They shake hands and smile. Kids curtsey. The same all over town. No wonder Mother stays away from here where normal human beings live and talk, touch and smile.

We are not the only butcher in town. This one has a pretty sign above his door of a carved cow, painted black and white with a yellow daisy in her mouth. Inside there is the butcher smiling at the shoppers who crowd his store, and for one short moment he turns, and I see his apron. It is white and clean, and I have an epiphany. Being a butcher's daughter or a butcher's wife is bad only if the butcher is bad.

Other stores have pretty signs as well. It's carrots and spinach for the green- grocer, a boot for the shoemaker, a snake for the apothecary. There are flower boxes below the windows and hanging baskets above. There's a happiness in the air. It is contagious. I look at babies in their carriages outside the stores, sleeping, crying, or red in the face pooping ones. I want to walk and meet neighbors, be part of this town. Many seem to know each other well. You can tell by the many handshakes, curtsies and smiles. Our town is pretty because people make it so. They shape the town much as if loving a person or one's home.

In a side street, kids from my school play ball. I quickly pedal past them, ignoring their calls to stop and play, too much in a hurry to get home.

We are separated from the town by the main road that connects neighboring towns with each other. The small road into town is right across from our store. It is mostly one large circle which meanders around, a squishy circle with stores in the center and homes lined up around it on smaller streets weaving in and out like patterns of a doily. Our house next to the main road is what brings us so much business from passing strangers and truckers, and why I never see anybody I know from school. We have a large sign on the store 'HANS UND LORE FLEISCHER'.

People must know our name, but maybe we are too filthy for them to shop.

They kind of must know Mother if for no other reason than for being weird. When she walks to get potatoes, she slouches, walks like a thief who doesn't want to be seen and never makes eye contact. If, on rare occasions, someone from town comes to shop in our store, she asks me to help while Father....

I never thought about it before. He hides his face and retreats into the butchery. He must have a secret. For the first time, I wonder what it is.

Frau Rittenmaier provides me with many books. I hide them in my room, read them and return them for new ones.

"Bring me books of families and love, nothing scary, please."

At night, I read instead of sleeping until my eyes hurt and I fall into a deep slumber. In the morning, Mother calls me with her low and raspy voice.

"Get your ass down here, don't bother with breakfast, damn you."

More and more it hurts me to listen to their nasty talk. It always seemed to be normal, and I dread to think that I might still use such language myself since I am not always sure what is bad and why. Mother angers me more than Father who is truly evil and enjoys it, while she is evil only when he is around, as if she must hurt me to please him. Hers is not an excuse!

More and more they want my help in the store, even in the morning before I leave for school. They don't need my help;

they only want to hold me back. Dumb bastards! Don't they know I am already smarter than they are?

Father cuts the meats and Mother and I arrange it on large platters. After school, I take people's money, wrap the meats, clean the floors with a big broom. Its coarse bristles never remove the filth. I guess Mother washes it sometimes or it would be slippery. Some men spit their tobacco juice into the spittoon from a distance like it's a sport and the greenish goo misses and drops on the floor. Those I single out for a generous amount of my own spit. When they don't watch, I spit in my hands and rub it around their meat while wrapping it in paper. Extra moist with no charge. Bastards!

"You are getting on in years," Father blurts out in anger one morning. "I'll take you out of school, all that fucking learning is twisting your mind. My friend's boy is ready to marry. You're lucky he lusts after a cunt like yours."

I notice Mother's bird face. She is upset. That new word must be worse than all the others. I must remember it. Maybe call him a cunt one day!

"Yes, Father," I say and keep going to school. Better not stir the pot until it needs stirring. And I know I am much too young to marry. He is the dumb old cunt.

We are not normal, that much I know. Breathing is barely allowed unless it's done to yell obscenities. And I still fear for my life every day when running to the outhouse in case one of the vicious Rottweilers should get loose. They follow me into my dreams where they growl and attack me. My own muffled screams wake me up in a puddle of sweat, pulse racing.

The dogs and Father and Mother scare away any living and decent thing. Only the ants used to bring life to me. They were my pets. I watched them work together and help each other. I know they did. Big or small we all have a life, and a big fat bastard like Father should not be in the way of mine. HE should get butchered. For the first time, I dare to have such a thought. I like it. The butcher needs butchering. Turn him into sausages.

5

TAKING CHANCES

At ten years of age, the time has come to decide whether to continue grade school or take the test to go on to high school. I try to sign up for the test.

"Your parents have to sign for you," I am told.

"They won't, but I want to go."

"Life doesn't work that way, deary, go get one of their signatures."

Stupid lady, damn her, her big glasses and hair like a poodle! What a cunt!

I don't know their signatures and create one that looks mean and spooky enough to be theirs. Nobody notices and I go take the test. It is easy and I am done early and tell the poodle lady to send the results to Frau Rittenmaier's house. At recess, I tell Frau Rittenmaier.

"For heaven's sake, Klara, why did you do that? Your parents need to know, you must inform them, they are your parents!"

I look at her, plead with her. She doesn't care.

"I will come with you and tell them."

"Please don't. They don't know about the piano playing either."

"They don't? Then where have you been practicing?"

"Here at recess with you, and now with Frau Graf."

She looks at me rolling her eyes and shoulders like 'what's the matter with you, girl.'

"Klara. You can't get away with it, you need to tell me what's going on."

I say nothing, and another nothing and more of the same but look at her with the intensity of a glaring fire. It is a matter of life and death, I might burn alive if Father finds out, and she listens to my silence.

"It's not my home." I finally said it.

"Not your home? But, but where..?"

"It's not my home, they are not my parents. Please let me just see if I even get into high school. They want me to stop learning and marry a butcher. Please give me that chance."

"Who are they?"

"I don't know." And with that, it's out in the air and cannot be stuffed back.

About a week later, Frau Rittenmaier meets me at recess.

"Klara, you passed the test with flying colors. On a more serious note, how are you going to handle it with your parents? High school will take much more of your time, they will notice."

"I don't know yet. But please, please let me go to school for as long as possible."

She looks at me, sad and worried, puts her hand on my

shoulder and almost talks but shakes her head instead, and I quickly leave.

Instead of going straight home I take a long leisurely detour, want to see the whole town, watch more closely how people live and mostly, I want to clear my brain before returning to the turmoil and danger that will be awaiting me. I will be very late, and I will start high school. What will happen to me? I pedal slowly, steadily, going further and further, meander around the small streets and houses with flowers on their windowsills, metal bars in the back yards for brushing rugs. There are gardens every-where and gooseberry bushes, currants and hazelnuts, fruit trees, a couple of chairs or a bench to sit on. There are swings hanging on tree branches, jump ropes and balls. If only they were mine. I keep an old sock, stuffed with other old socks, and use it like a ball. It doesn't bounce but I throw it up and catch it. Throw it up around my back and from under my leg. Throw it up and hit it with my head or elbow and catch it. How pitiful. There is a whole world out there, mine to discover. I drive past city hall and the little blue library, peddle into a park right behind it with beautiful large trees and a small pond. There is a hill behind the park. I wonder how far up it goes. One day I shall find out.

The sun is starting to set when I approach our house, a deadly fear gripping me. My brain got not at all cleared but feels swollen and lethargic. 'Armageddon,' I hear myself whis-per. It's going to happen. I quietly enter the store and start to shake. There are no customers.

"Hello." My voice is cracking.

Mother enters first, her dark eyes burning with an intensity I have never seen in her. It's a deadly fear for her life and maybe for mine. When Father enters behind her, ready to explode and inflict grave bodily harm, she leans into the wall and cowers in front of him, the chickenhearted bitch and the big bad bully. He kicks her away, grabs me, twists my arm with his small hand and slaps me around, then loosens his grip to take off his belt for the vicious, dangerous out of control beating. That's what gives him real pleasure. I remember those. Mother will be next, and she won't do anything about it.

On the counter next to me is the big meat cleaver. I grab it and throw it at him with uncontrolled anger. It hits him in the thigh, and he screams in pain. I wish I had killed him, truly wish I had.

"That's the last time you hit me you damn shit. I know your secret, you fucking bastard!

"Secret? What secret?" He asks, writhing in pain. I smell his fear. It is how animals smell in line for getting butchered and with the same burning yet blank expression.

"The reason you can't show your face, why you go out only in the dark. I passed the test for high school. I play the piano and am giving a concert soon. People know you are not my parents. But they don't know that you stole me. I'll keep both your secrets if you behave."

Will they notice that I am bluffing, know that cold terror filled me with those words?

Mother and Father are ashen. Both stare at me in panic. I scared them! Yes. I did and I lied. There is no concert planned, I am not that good.

"How did you learn his secret?" Mother hisses like a poisonous snake, spittle shooting out of her mouth.

"One can learn a lot if one is smart."

They don't question me any further. They believe that I know, and that's all that matters. She cleans his wound with iodine and his howls of pain please me. What a crybaby! It's a good deep cut, and the cleaver was not very clean. He should see a doctor.

"I hope you die and rot in hell."

"Shut up," Mother yells, "You were lucky."

"He was the lucky one, Mother."

That night, I go to bed with the door locked and sleep underneath my bed should he break the door and come storming in.

His wails, his moans and groans keep me awake, each sound a drop of balm on my ears. Fucking bastard got some of his own medicine. I finally fall asleep into a world of violent thunderstorms shaking the house, lightning blinding my eyes, walls collapsing around me. Father is running away, his unkempt yellow hair flaps in the wind, a girl's tiny nightgown covers his fleshy shoulders, and his blubbery smelly ass hangs low and is butt naked.

It's around that time that one of the Rottweilers goes missing. No, I don't 'miss' him. One is terrifying enough on the daily walks to the outhouse. But for the first time I wonder how any dog can be kind if he is chained and caged. Or any person. And a powerful stirring inside my heart reminds me that once I was loved, was surrounded by love. It is a voice rather than a memory, and I repeat it many times over. I was loved. Let me never forget, please God, let me never forget that once I was loved!

If I forget I'd be like them, unlovable.

6

PARENTS, PERIODS AND PREGNANCY

Winter is speeding along crashing into Spring. Old age will gobble up my youth before I lived it properly. All those wasted years, what a pity. I help in the store when he works in the back, read my books when he is in the store. We do not look at each other. I say: 'good morning,' and 'good night,' and he grunts things under his breath and his small hands have not threatened me again. But he is a volcano, lying dormant before exploding and crushing Mother and me.

Easter has passed. High school will start tomorrow in the next town over, about an extra fifteen minutes on my bike. It is a new beginning with new teachers and kids from other small surrounding towns. I don't have a reputation yet for being weird and would like to keep it that way. Mother sewed me a couple of new dresses made of brand-new fabric. I scared them alright and am proud. The more they are scared the less I fear them.

"I want you to have a good start," she said, then threw the clothes at me in anger.

"Thank you, Mother, I am grateful and...

"Oh, stuff it. We both know how we feel, you and I."

"Thank you anyway. They are pretty, and I mean it."

And they are, and it is a good start. Clothes should not make such a difference, but they do.

With Father being a spineless chicken, I take many liberties. Frau Graf gives me private lessons at her own place now, still without charge. Every Wednesday you'll see me pedal to her house, walk up to her apartment into her living room and straight to the black concert grand piano. We awaken it together, she and I, this black wild animal, with our four hands and a fiery piece that sweeps over the house into the yard, and the sound swoops up the birds as they soar into the sky. It dazzles me every time anew and, to do it justice, I practice harder than ever on the virtual piano in the corner of my tiny room.

On Mondays and Thursdays there are classes after school for those that want some extra learning. I enroll in a special writing class and a geology class without asking Mother and Father. The extra freedom, the time to read and to learn, it's a miracle and I soak it up like a sponge, no matter what it is.

When I stop by Frau Rittenmaier's house, she always likes the surprise.

"How do you like high school? How is it going at home now?"

She gives me a dress she doesn't wear any more. It's getting too tight in the front and she is afraid a button might inappropriately pop during class.

"It's not really your color, you would look better in green," she says.

"It's perfect. Blue is my favorite color. Light blue with the red of spilled blood. A memory goes with these colors."

The teakettle is hissing. Frau Rittenmaier pours the hot water into a little blue teapot for two, covers it with a blue hand crocheted tea cozy, gets two delicate teacups with white and blue flowers to match, and we sit down at a table in a little alcove covered in a last splash of sunlight. She has a slender neck and her movements are graceful without Frau Graf's excess energy as she fills our cups with mint tea.

Outside, snow bells and crocuses peek out between patches of crisp white snow. Soon the smell of lilacs will attract the first insects.

"Your yard is amazing, like an oasis. Our snow is filthy and covered in garbage, and it always smells of death. Even our rats would leave if it weren't for the easy scraps of meat."

"Klara, I can't wait to hear your story. It sounds too awful to keep to yourself. It would be safe with me if you trust me enough."

It takes me a while to think about. "I do trust you. But if you have ever been on a sinking boat not wanting to jump off quite yet, then you'll understand."

"Oh, Klara, I am so sorry. Remember, I'll be here when the time comes."

There is a girl in my class, Isabel, gentle like Frau Rittenmaier and strong willed like Frau Graf. I would love so much to be her friend, learn from her, get answers to my life's questions.

One day I watch her enter Frau Graf's house.

"Do you take piano lessons?" I ask her the next day.

"Yes. Do you?"

"I do, and I love everything about her."

Isabel is not so sure. "She always pushes me to practice more," she complains.

"Do you have your own piano?"

She looks at me quizzically, a princess in a fairy tale with her amazingly blue eyes, white skin and straight blond hair waved at the bottom.

"Of course, how else could I learn it. Don't you have one?"

I don't want to lie and brag about the imagined piano in my room, which, by the way, has grown into a grand piano and barely fits even as a figment of my imagination.

"It's tricky, it's I don't know, we ...." I take a deep breath. "No, I don't have a piano."

"How do you practice? There are rumors that you are good."

"I practice during my lesson. And in my mind. I drew the keyboard on a large sheet of butcher paper and practice with my eyes closed. I can feel the mistakes and hear the sour notes."

"No way! How can you feel the keys without keys and hear their sound without a sound? Can you come home with me after school and show me?"

My heart skips a beat. I am outrageously happy. My first visit to another student's home and I didn't even have to ask.

"I would love to."

I follow her on my bike on which I can comfortably sit now. She lives between Frau Graf and Frau Rittenmaier, not far from either one, in a little house inside a garden with winter vegetables. Orange curtains with bright flowers add a touch of spring. A small bike is in our path to the front door, and a small truck and a soccer ball are strewn around. It does not look messy but rather friendly. Our mess is old and greasy, nasty looking, uninviting. Her Mother opens the door before we even ring the bell. She comes out all the way, delighted to see us.

"And who is this lovely lady?" she asks, smiling at me while hugging Isabel and slapping a noisy kiss on her cheek. I could cry from envy.

"It's Klara. She plays the piano but doesn't have one to practice or play on."

We shake hands and I curtsey, and she quickly closes the door behind me to keep the warm air in. When Isabel takes off her shoes, I follow her example because of the role model thing. Her Mama hands me an extra pair of slippers. Her name is Frau Dietrich and she looks like Isabel with slightly darker hair and barely older. They could be sisters. She fixes us some rye bread with butter, puts a bit of honey on it and gives us each a very wrinkly apple from the garden, the last of last year's crop.

"They are like people," she says. "They get wrinkly with age but oh so sweet."

She has a dimple in her chin. I like her very much. With a loud, high pitched sound, Isabel's little brother Nicholas comes running in. A cheerful boy, clever looking with his freckled face hiding under a crop of reddish curls. His eyes sparkle with mischief. Well-loved is how I see it. In a moment, he is back out the door with another high-pitched sound.

"He thinks he is some kind of a bird or airplane, different every day but reliably noisy," explains Frau Dietrich.

Isabel hands me her music. It's an easy piece and I ask if I may play from another book that says: 'Chopin Waltzes.'

"It's Mama's. Isn't it too hard since you don't have a piano?"

I don't answer but look for a fast and happy piece because

that's how I feel right now, and I decide on Opus 64 #1 in D-flat major, also called the 'Minute Waltz.' To tell the truth it takes me longer than a minute to play. My fingers take off flying. A gusty spring breeze outside dances along, cleaning and spreading the last of winter's dirt. I am too absorbed to notice Isabel's Mother breathing down my neck.

"You must have a piano." She sounds astonished.

"I don't. I never did." And my tears and my nose start running from a deep well of sadness and I wipe it all with my sleeve, make a snotty mess, grab my bag and run out the door.

"Thank you," I mumble but don't know if they even heard me.

The next day I cannot go to school, am still too overwhelmed and sickened from strong emotions.

"Are you sick?" asks Mother.

"I don't know. I feel shaky and my stomach hurts."

She stands at the door for a while, like wanting to say something.

"What is it?" I say. "Don't just stand there."

"You might be getting your period. Do you know what that is?" I don't.

"At around your age, it's normal for girls to bleed once a month. You might feel cramps in your stomach."

What is she babbling about, the old goat! She comes a few steps closer. She has not done that since I was very little, when she sang to me with her raspy voice when he was not home.

"It gets your body ready to have babies."

I sit up with a jolt. "I might have a baby then?"

"Only if you are with a man in bed and he gets you pregnant."

"You sleep with Father and never get pregnant."

'Oh God' I think, 'what if it did happen?'

"I once was."

She has a strange distant look, her face like a mask. Why is she telling me this now? As if in a trance, she backs out of my room looking almost pretty if it weren't for that pinched grimace of hers and the beady eyes of a vulture. I am astounded and disturbed. Could she have lost a child and snatched me in its stead?

Her answers beget more questions. Why do I get pregnant with a man in my bed? He must do something other than snore and fart. Besides, I like my own bed. And could it happen on a sofa? It makes no sense to need a bed. And what if I suddenly bleed in the middle of geometry class? How much blood will there be, and does it come out of my nose like when Father used to slap me? Or will it gush out of my mouth or down from where I pee, and I'll be bleeding all over like getting butchered? She is not telling me all there is, the stupid goat. Nothing makes sense.

I follow her into the kitchen where she sits at the table, her face in her hands, convulsing with soundless sobs and tears that stay dry, her body rocking.

"What is it? Would you like some water?"

"Go away. It's all too late."

"I need to know about the bleeding. Where does it come out and what do I do? I don't want a child. Look at me, I AM a child."

She does not answer, does not look at me. She sits still now, forgetting to breathe, staring straight ahead, an almost corpse being eaten alive by her own rotting soul. I look around our kitchen and notice for the first time its bleakness. I could clean up the dirt and put order into this mess, but it wouldn't be enough. We need new walls, new people and a different air to breathe and why can't she repair the curtain and hang it back up properly? It's been torn and crooked since I live here. It's embarrassing. I go back upstairs and look around my room. It's not as bad. When I feel better, I'll clean it and keep it that way. Don't want to live like they do, filthy vermin.

Later in the evening she comes up with a plate of meat and potatoes. Once before, a long time ago now, when I was sick and feverish, she brought me a bowl of soup and left it on the wooden stand; never came back up to check on me. She must have thought I'd come back down on my own if I live, else it would not matter anyways.

"The bleeding will happen between your legs," she explains. "I'll buy you what you need. As for a child, just don't be alone with a man."

Those words keep haunting me. Why, why for heaven's sake can't I be alone with a man? It seems that the bleeding is related to babies and that my nose plays no part. Maybe Frau Rittenmaier will tell me more.

Next day, feeling well again, I visit Frau Rittenmaier after school. She is pregnant with twins and so fat she waddles like a duck in her husband's huge beige sweater, and if anybody knows how to get pregnant, she'd be the one to ask. Her husband is a teacher also, and when she talks about him her eyes light up with love and such longing that I can't, just can't ask her.

Am I embarrassed? Too private? I am not shy any longer, just a bit removed like an observer rather than a participant of the life around me. Wish I could grab life the way I grab piano keys. Wish I'd learn all about table manners, small talk, what's appropriate at my age. I have finally mastered not to say any of the words used in my house. Well, mostly.

"You'll be a role model soon to my kids!" She reminded me the other day when I used a certain vile word. "If they start to talk like you, I'll spank YOU, not them."

Then we laughed.

No, I can't ask her, just can't. And she wonders why I stare and not say a word and leave again.

7

CONCENTRATION CAMPS. REALLY?

Spring has turned to summer and summer into autumn since I learned about babies. Or did I? It still makes no sense and when something doesn't seem right it usually isn't. I like boys and they like me, but I can't see getting pregnant simply by being alone with one. However, with Harald I feel a giddiness that turns me into soft mush. My knees buckle. And when I feel his eyes follow me, I get unhinged and walk with wobbly legs. When he's done playing soccer, his pungent sweat fuels in me a ravenous new kind of fierce hunger. I want to grab him, lick him and bite him, something, anything physical. It drives me mad. We are two magnets that want to touch; and my tongue - if you ever saw an overheated dog - mine hangs out nearly as far whenever I see him. When he talks, I giggle. I never giggle. But I giggle. Maybe that's part of it, the part that leads to having babies.

Time moves on. I skip along on the slow journey to find my place in life, am still the little runt, tiny and skinny. Harald and

I have been talking quite often for the last few months. He likes to talk about books and homework and other things, and I try not to giggle too much like a silly girl. He thinks I am smart. Lately he tells me about his Father who died in the war, and he tells me about the war itself. Why does nobody else talk about it? Harald mentions atrocities so horrible that I have a hard time believing him. Wouldn't the teachers know and why don't they talk about it? I start asking questions in school and notice their hesitation. They do know things but don't want to tell. No, it couldn't have happened, not here in Germany!

And yet. Could it be true?

Today at school, my classmates serenaded me for my fifteenth birthday. Even Herr Stahl, the physics teacher sang along with a surprisingly beautiful tenor voice. It touched me to tears. My emotions turn on their heel at a moment's notice. Joy and sorrow are my dearest friends and I never know which one will respond.

Isabel planned a small party for me at her house. It's where I practice the piano now and savor new and delicious meals. Her Mama always invites me for the midday meal after school. It's amazing all the things one can eat besides meat and potatoes.

It's a small party and we play board games. I don't know any of them and feel, once again, like an outsider. I don't even know 'Mensch Ärgere Dich Nicht' which, they swear, every self-respecting German knows. It's a game which attempts to get you angry; but getting angry is against the rules. Then we eat cheesecake with the last blackberries from their garden. I stole bunches of lunch meat from the store as a gift for Frau Dietrich. Later, I'll bring some to Harald's Mother because she can't stand me. Maybe she will like me then. He gave me a little book with romantic poems and an inscription 'from Harald with love to Klara, my dearest friend.'

Yes, we go out together now, go to the movies when he has money or for walks in the park when he doesn't. We hold hands when we walk through town, his fingers slowly weaving their way around mine like a zipper and, once we enter the park and nobody looks, we kiss. We kiss till my legs get so limp they're nearly lifeless, and my heart races and I don't know where his tongue starts and mine stops and then I want him so badly for something, like squeezing him to death till I find a way to crawl inside of him. Then I'll nibble my way back out. Always he stops when it gets so good and tells me he loves me. I wish he didn't stop but that's what happens. We don't know what else to do. His mother still hates me despite the lunchmeats, stupid old bitch.

I have become a popular girl without my doing. They are intrigued by the secrets surrounding me. I share nothing of my life, not even with Harald, since I am still a stranger to myself, and he has sadly stopped talking about the war now that it has piqued my interest. I don't know why but suddenly it seems urgent to learn more about it. After all, I was stolen during the war! Maybe somewhere I can find a tiny grain of truth, a secret connection to my shadows.

    I think I love him too, but also get aroused by other boys. There are so many. Young men look me up and down and I feel their eyes follow me. Their whistles embarrass and entice, make me wonder how their kisses would taste and their touches would feel.

. . .

A cool breeze is blowing bare the trees, their colorful leaves floating gently to the ground. A perfect winter cover for snails, slugs and earwigs to hide and keep warm. Nature takes care of its creatures except for me, I guess. And I pity myself shamelessly, a pleasure pity of sorts. 'It is what it is,' they say. For me, in such moments, 'it is what it was.' And I hold on to my shadows with all my might the way one would hold on to a rope over a bottomless pit.

Eight months ago, Frau Rittenmaier gave births to twins, Josef and Martina, and I finally met her husband, a man as warm and inviting as she is, with the same brown eyes and roundish face. But where she has hair, he is mostly bald. A few long strands of hair which he combs over don't help much, and there is a soft brown fuzz around the back and very bushy eyebrows. The rest seems to grow like weeds in his ears and down on his chest where it peeks out over the top button of his shirt and down his strong arms when he pulls up his sleeves.

I often stop by, even just for two seconds like today. Babies are awfully cute. Last week we had the time of our lives rolling in leaves and in the smells of fall, a first for the babies and me.

I give the door a good knock. "Right there." The door opens with Frau Rittenmaier holding her twins. I grab Josef for a hug and kiss, nozzle his neck and inhale its sweetness. He spits up and 'yuck,' I hand him back in exchange for Martina who badly needs a fresh diaper.

"Come on in, there's a better smell in the kitchen," she laughs out loud while taking back Martina. It's one of her delicious cakes, which she bakes every week for Sunday afternoon coffee time, and I step inside just for a moment.

. . .

"I need to learn about Stalin, Hitler, the war and those camps. All I know is from rumors, innuendos and whispers. Even teachers are worried to talk about it and I need to know especially about the camps."

"Ach Klara!" She sighs. "Look, the enormity of what happened has not set in. If you look at a large painting from too close you cannot see it. It's the same with history. It takes time."

"Mainly it's the Nazis in the government that don't want us to know," shouts Herr Rittenmaier from the kitchen. "We should have shot them all."

I agree from the little I know about it and would love to stay but grab the door.

"I got to go and do this."

"Klara, I won't mind talking about the war and the camps, really I won't. It will be terribly hard doing it on your own."

"I'll think about it, I promise." I blow some kisses towards the twins, make a funny face, yell 'thank you' and get going.

Nothing new in any newspapers at our little blue library. Should have stayed for a piece of Streuselkuchen. Or was it an apple cake?

Father's bloodshot eyes stare at me when I come home, a dangerous glint in his usually dull eyes. It has been a long time without us talking or looking at each other. He frightens me again. His fat stomach fills the doorway. I don't want to squeeze by his blubber with the filthy apron and the stench from his crotch and stop below the two stone steps to the entry, the hair on my skin standing up.

"You are late!" He looks me over as if he saw me for the first time, the way some men look at me lately, his feverish eyes secretly undressing me. A cold shiver makes me trip over my own feet.

"Where is Mother?" He barely points his head towards town.

I take my bike and turn around. She can't be far. And here she is around the corner, her shopping bag heavy with potatoes. It is a relief to see the old bitch and I stop to hang the bag on my bike.

"Mother, he gives me the willies. Don't leave me alone with the lecherous ass."

"I know how you feel."

"Did something happen? Did he get drunk?"

"He went to his friends last night, came back very late in a crazy state of mind. I swear he'll kill us someday soon."

Mother is more scared than I am. Her steps are so timid she is trying to avoid the ground altogether. Her low voice, stuck in her throat, sounds like a caged bullfrog. We turn the corner and he is waiting, biding his time. He hates when we talk, and we stop our whispers. At the door, he steps aside for us. We enter.

Nothing happens but everything has changed. I smell it and keep checking behind my back, behind my own shadow.

Every day now I drive to the big library after school to check newspapers, driven by an urgency that defies reason. More and more articles pop up.

Finally, I find a map of those camps, hidden away as if on purpose in an unmarked binder. There was one not far from where we live. I've heard people call them death camps, like our butchery but for people. Harald was right. They did exist. Father used to work in that direction and come home on weekends. The Russians were marching towards Berlin at the time, and maybe that's where all those legs were running from, thousands of them, amongst them my shadow family. Mother could have snatched me and run south, not too far for her to do in a couple of days, or with help. But why?

So many questions. Books are still waiting to be written. They will take time and distance to gain proper perspective, I get it now. Close-up you see too many details to connect the dots. Over the next weeks I find more news but not what I am looking for.

Until today.

It's an article about the camp near us, one of the worst. Guards did more than follow orders. They found pleasure in torturing and doctors were monsters and experimented on humans. Photos of starved men, women and children, their large eyes lit with the last flicker of a flame before being snuffed out. My blood boils. There were ovens and gas chambers here in Germany. A shame overcomes me, a shame so deep I want to scream and hide, crushed under this new unbearable burden of being me, a German, then feel a sudden gratitude for my own miserable life. After a few deep breaths, I begin to think. There is nothing I can do about the past. I must quickly leave it behind me, must bundle my grief into a tight knot in my stomach to be untangled when the time is right. If I let it eat me alive now, Father will kill me. I am certain he is guilty of something horrible and certain that time is running out.

8

A STROKE, AND SAUSAGES OF ALL KINDS

A loud crash and bang startles me out of my sleep. Somebody fell hard, wall-shakingly hard. I jump out of bed into the dark and cold night, sit down on the top step of the old squeaky stairs. There is no sound. Once, I tried sliding down the railing. Got a threshing for it and a deep splinter on the inside of my thigh.

Then it starts, a low moaning, a groaning, and I go downstairs in a terror, step by slow step, gripping the railing, walk to their bedroom and touch the doorknob. I am not allowed inside, have never entered or even peeked into this room. I let go of the knob and walk back to the kitchen counter to get a knife. At least I'll have a fighting chance. Then I go and open the door.

The light is on. Mother is on the floor trembling, twitching, half her face drooping down, a lifeless, empty bag, saliva dripping from the corner of her twisted mouth.

"She is having a stroke," says Father, turning over trying to go back to sleep.

"Get your fat ass up and get her to the hospital," I shout, throwing his smelly clothes on his face and pulling the blanket off the bed. Oh, God, the stench! And he is truly butt naked, his nightgown having crawled up to above his hairy back.

"Damn piece of shit," he shouts and farts right into my face with a long low rumble like cannon fire and I jump back, traumatized by this mean man. How I would love to strangle and butcher him till he is more dead than a corpse, watch rats feast on his sorry cadaver, but I need to take control as the only adult around here.

"There is new information about the camp where you worked," I yell.

He gets up as fast as he can which is very slow. The vast amount of ass, belly and breasts like a woman's seems to anchor him to the bed.

"You'll soon be too fat to get up. I won't be bringing you food then, but I'll send the rats to feed on you."

He finally stands upright, picks up Mother and carries her to the old rusty truck and throws her in the back. Yes. Throws her like a bag of rags. I climb in after her and lean her head on my shoulder and try to hold it steady. A disgusting thing to do, but she is a little bit of a Mother, a terrible, wicked Mother, but infinitely better than the cruel stinky Nazi. That's what he is, a Nazi. I finally learned what it means.

"Hurry, I say."

At the emergency room entry, I hurry in and call the nurses. When they rush out Father has his hat over his face, pretending to sleep. They get Mother out of the truck and help her in. I come along. A young tired doctor with a large burn mark on his face checks her out behind a curtain while a young nurse asks me questions from behind a desk. I don't have any answers. She wants me to get Father.

"He has the flu," I lie, "he is outside vomiting, can we do it another day? He is the butcher in town." She nods her head and keeps typing.

"It was a stroke," says the doctor moments later, "a minor one but there could be more. She needs to stay in the hospital. Come back tomorrow during visiting hours." For a second he looks through my nightgown which is threadbare and probably see through. I feel naked and ashamed.

Back in the truck, Father grunts his sounds and squeezes out his farts, and we drive home. I run upstairs, lock my door and rush under my warm feather blanket, shivering from the cold and the fear.

The next morning is a Saturday, a holiday and no school. After a bite of blood sausage for breakfast I put on my apron and go to work in the store. Father is lethargic. I imagine him using a wheelbarrow soon to wheel his bloated stomach along. What a disgusting asshole. The pig would have let her die last night!

What would I do without Mother, or rather what would I do with him alone? I wouldn't, couldn't. If she dies, I need to go tell my story at once. I hoped to wait till I am old enough to be on my own. What exactly is my story? A blue dress with blood and no last name? Piano playing? Legs running? And my fake Father who smells bad of something besides his normal repulsive stench. Can I tell my story yet? And to whom? What if I am wrong?

I put meats on the platters, get the cash register ready, put out the 'OPEN' sign, and wipe the glass top. He watches me with that lecherous look. I feel him undressing me in his mind. What shall I do? I can't leave yet, Mother needs me.

There are not many customers this morning. For the midday meal, I make a pot of coffee and we both grab some lunchmeats. He makes the kitchen too small a place to share, and I take my food upstairs. When the bell rings to announce a customer, I run down, give him what he wants and take his money, count it quickly before he runs back out.

As soon as the door closes Father comes back in, stands right behind me, puts his bloody hands on my front and I can't run. Thousands of tiny insects with sharp legs crawl over my skin from fear. He has never touched me unless it was to cause pain. My screams don't come out and no one would hear them. He squeezes me hard against the glass counter with its meats and sausages, trying to suffocate me with his arms and the stink from his mouth in my neck. He pulls my apron over my head and lets it drop on the floor, takes off his own apron and throws it on top of mine. I don't want our aprons to touch, want to kick them apart, their closeness is agitating me more than his touch. But I am a wisp of a girl cornered by this bull. His left arm grips me around my breasts while his right slips into the soft waistband of my skirt. He rubs my belly as if in a gentle caress.

"Good girl," he whispers in my ear. "Good girl."

A cold terror grips me, wish he'd call me 'shit,' it would be familiar and safe. I am stiff from fear as his filthy fingers move to where my hair has grown into a small bush. He rubs and keeps rubbing there and between my legs, and I can't recognize what it is I feel, this cold terror and revulsion and a certain electricity, and why is he gentle? Why doesn't he beat me and cut and hurt me? I become detached from myself and find a strange calm.

I watch me be. One of my frizzy hairs is getting stuck on his filthy fingernail and it hurts when he moves his hand. I am glad for the pain. I am one of his animals and will get butchered, and it will all be over. It is quite pleasant really. A kitten found a sunny spot on top of our truck, a dog barks and another one answers. Flies shit on our meat. It's all as it should be. The picture on the wall, I've never actually seen it under its layers of spider webs and dead bugs. I will take it down when this is over and clean it, clean everything around me and uncover the truth beneath the turds.

He is fiddling with his own pants. I can't see it but feel him opening the buttons in front. His right hand reaches back down to my bush. He calls it by a strange name like the kitten on the truck while his left lets go of my breasts to hold up his stomach. Now he pushes against me with his privates. There seems to grow a sausage on him that's trying to wiggle its way into me. Like the sausages in front of me on the counter. They are large, made especially for truckers. 'Big Boys' we call them. 'Big Bad Boys' say some of the truckers while leering at me. All they are is dead meat stuffed into skins. Like Father and Mother. We all are nothing but sausages. How would we taste, sweet or peppery?

Why is nobody coming? Where are the truckers? All I see and smell are sausages. Wieners, frankfurters and pork sausages and his, sticking out from his crotch.

"Bend down," he whispers, and I bend. "Good girl, a bit more, more, more," his voice getting loud and impatient, and I bend far down with his hand on my bush, my hands on the floor, and his thing rubbing against my skirt. With one big swoop, he pulls skirt and panties down to my ankles and lets his crotch with the slimy sausage rub against my bare skin. It is so gross it startles me out of my stupor. I need to fight before it's too late. His fat arm has loosened its grip enough that I can turn my head and snap at it with raw rage. Bite into it for my life, must bite through the skin to hold on to him, feel blood in my mouth, want to vomit, want to kick and scream and die, but I keep on biting deep down through thick leathery skin, my teeth weaponized into sharp tools like those he used on me when I was just a little girl, and I use the strength and passion I learned from Frau Graf. 'Bite harder, girl, bite with courage.' I hear her voice loud and clear and take out a real bite like our Rottweiler would if he were not chained. I cannot let go or I'll be dead meat, good enough as stuffing for a Big Boy! How many sausages could he stuff with my meat? How much money is my life worth?

At this very moment, I know for sure that life has better plans for me.

He lets go of a howling scream just in time when a customer enters. It's a trucker who doesn't care who is screaming or why. Father limps to the back holding up his pants, blood gushing from his arm, yelling obscenities that would make other truckers run to church and pray, or at least help me. But not this one. I quickly pull up my skirt and panties, serve him what he asks for, take his money with trembling fingers, drop all the coins from shaking so hard. They dance along the counter with their pitiful clacking clinking noises. Clang, clack, click! I open the cash register and laugh, can't stop laughing, and instead of putting the money in I empty it out and stuff my pockets, then run in panic out the door right behind the trucker. I get on my bike and feel a wetness in my panties. The pig must have pissed on me. I spit out what's left between my teeth of his rotten flesh, then pedal towards the hospital to Mother.

But my mind is too agitated to visit, and my body is in turmoil. The vision of human sausages, of me a cannibal, biting into Father whose taste might never leave my mouth is too much. How am I to be? I keep biking and biking, at a total loss of who I am, what just happened, how to think about it. I hear myself cry and swear and cry lots more with long periods of nothing. A total blank. What I know is never to go back there.

When the sun's shadows grow long, I finally enter the hospital and Mother's room. She looks dead and peaceful, better as a corpse than I've ever seen her look alive. It must have just happened. They wouldn't leave a corpse in a room, would they? I touch her arm. It is heavy, dangles down cold and stiff. One part of her face is still droopy. With trembling hands, I sit and take her hand in mine. She jerks it away. I freak out and jump. She fooled me, the stupid goat, and I feel enraged and ready to leave.

"Ach, cha, rch, ch, rach." She makes guttural sounds, grunts and snorts like a pig in labor, her haunted eyes open now, misty from long forgotten tears, and she looks straight at me. Could it be? Is she trying to tell me something? I sit back down. What a pitiful creature she is in her hospital gown, a tiny bird swallowed up by the pillows. Her arm has the look of a freshly butchered chicken leg still jerking about with its last bit of life force, and I grab her hand with both of mine. She lets me hold it, heaving with quick little sobs.

. . .

Her cold hand takes me back to the many desolate winters. Those were the worst of times. The beautiful snow that I learned to dread from the agony of having no mittens or socks. Not for lack of but as punishment. I was stranded in my room for days on end, too cold to sit outside and touch the snow while it was clean. And I move my hand away from Mother for her coldness and callousness. Why should she need me when I need her more? I need her so much more and right now. My rage is coming back and the terror, want to take it out on her, want to hit her for Father's touch for she is guilty too. But a nurse comes, visiting hours are over and I must leave. What will become of me?

I bike through the night. Slowly, lights get turned off, a few stars appear behind clouds. I don't know what it all means. Her stroke, the stars, the panic and my pussy. That's what he called it! Like his little kitten. My bike takes me to Frau Rittenmaier. She is my truest friend and angel. I swallow my rage and terror into another tiny knot in my stomach. It's getting crowded in there. Then I knock at the door, a smile forced onto my face.

"Look who's here. What are you doing out so late, come on in?"

He sits back down. The kids fell asleep on the carpet. She sits on the sofa soaking her feet in a bucket of hot water.

She calls her husband 'Wolf,' and he calls her 'Schatz,' my treasure. And they love each other. I stare at the notion. It makes no sense. Nothing does.

"Did you have dinner?" She asks. How should I know? I can barely stand still without falling over from trembling so hard and my panties are still moist.

"Wolf, help her please and get her some food."

He limps over to me, gently takes my arm and guides me to the sofa. I drop down next to her and he goes to get a plate of pancakes. But I can't eat. He sits down on my other side and takes my hands, holds them in both of his.

"Start talking to us. You can spend the night." He is already in pajamas. They are striped, but I can't see the color, can't see any colors. It's all a blank.

And I cry and cry, puddles of tears, and I can't stop. I shake, I shudder, almost vomit from the fear, the sadness, the taste of Father.

9

KLARA'S STORY

"My story started a long time ago. I don't even know any longer whether it is a real story. I was four years old when my real family was running away amidst many other people. My real Mother wore light blue and blood was dripping from her head." And I tell them how my fake Mother snatched me, and how they beat me when I didn't want to change my name and my age. I called my real parents Mutti and Vati. "Those names and my own name, Monika, helped me hold on to myself and give some meaning to the shadows of my memory."

No matter how much crying one needs to do, there always comes the time when all tears are gone, all sobs have bubbled up, and all that's left is a raw tiredness inside the emptiness. And then comes the hunger. Ravenous like a starved animal, I gulp down the whole stack of pancakes with no regard to manners.

.   .   .

Herr Rittenmaier is picking up the twins, one at a time, kisses them before gently putting them down in their beds. Josef opens his eyes and closes them again with a little yelp. I watch and wonder, did ever anybody put me to bed so gently, so full of love? What is love? How does it even feel? I cannot feel anything, not even the rage.

When he is back, they ask about my parents here in town.

"Both are mean. She is cold, hard as ice, but he is vicious like the Rottweiler he keeps in chains. We used to have two, then one disappeared. He would have liked to kill me long ago, nobody would have known, maybe she didn't let him. He has a dirty secret. He hides under his hat and leaves the store when anybody comes in who might recognize him. I pretended to know his secret, told them others in town know that they are not my real parents, and that's why they let me go to high school.

"What happened today?"

"Mother had a stroke. She is in the hospital. I was alone with him."

"And?"

"He touched me. I bit him hard and ran away. The taste of his flesh, how will I ever wash it off?"

They exchange glances. He goes to check on the kids.

"Tell me, how did he touch you? Please tell me, don't be embarrassed with me, please, it's important."

"He squeezed me like one of those large snakes you know, like an anaconda. I bit and held on to his flesh for dear life."

"You must tell everything to the police." Herr Rittenmaier is back, and I feel a sudden nervous energy, a quick swap from terror into safety.

"I have something I need to do right now. Every week Father goes out in the dark, late when the moon is gone and few people are out, says he is seeing old friends. He comes back drunk and violent. It's dark now and he'll go tonight. I need to follow him to see who his friends are before going to the police. Maybe one of you can go with me?"

Herr Rittenmaier volunteers. He puts on a warm cardigan over his pajamas. Frau Rittenmaier hands him his coat and a very warm hat for his near baldness and bundles me into her winter coat, then ties a scarf around my head. It smells of her and I pull part of it over my face to breathe it in.

He follows me on his bike to where we can see my house. A single yellowish bulb shines a light, dull from dust and spider webs. The old truck sits on the dirt in front of the house. He won't see us.

"He always goes straight into town on this road."

We wait and wait, the cold burrowing into our bones. The sky is sprinkled with stars but no moon on this clear night. We are about to leave when I hear the faint screeching sound of our front door. He comes out, settles into the car and starts the engine. It coughs and sputters with nasty noises but even the diesel fumes smell better than he ever does. I begin to shake from nerves and the cold. We closely hug the wall of a building when he drives past us, then follow him. All these years Mother and I did not know where he was going. He stops almost at once at a small house. Its lights shine dimly through heavy curtains. It is around the corner from Herr and Frau Rittenmaier's house. Why does he even use a car? He knocks at the door. It hurriedly opens and swallows him without a word.

"Do you know who lives here?"

He shakes his head. "Maybe my wife does. She has lived here all her life." We pedal back as fast as we can to go ask her.

"Schatz," he calls quietly. The twins are asleep. Frau Rittenmaier, in a flowered nightgown, joins us at the dining table holding a tray with a pot of tea, three cups and sugar cubes. He describes the house to her. She pouts her lips into a perfect plum.

"There must be a mistake. Are you sure?" He repeats it.

"That's where the chief of police lives. How lucky you found out."

We drink our tea while it's hot and wonder what to do next. We can't go to the police chief if he is crooked.

"Isabel's Father is a police officer in the next town. Maybe he can help?" I say.

But Herr Rittenmaier is too exhausted to think. He puts a mattress out for me to sleep on and brings a blanket while she hands me a pillow. He always helps and her eyes are on him glowing with love. I don't think she even notices his limpy leg!

The lights off, the house quiet, my body can finally rest in a safe place and should let me fall into an easy sleep, but a sudden deadly fear grips my chest like a leaden weight. I can't breathe, hear noises around the house, and the stink of Father seeps through the door. He is coming close, ready to finish the job of what exactly is not clear. My own muffled screams wake me up. I toss and turn myself back into an uneasy sleep, dream of drowning, frantically try to move my arms that won't move, then grab ahold of the fleshy part of a dead animal. It's a sausage and it's disturbing. I let go of it and drown. Water enters my lungs. I wake up in a coughing fit and in a large puddle of pee, my arms still flailing around, agitated and deeply embarrassed that I ruined their mattress!

The very early morning light is barely breaking through the curtains. I hear faint gurgling sounds from the twins. What shall I do? I am getting cold in my own urine and don't have any other clothes to wear.

10

MOTHER'S STORY

Herr Rittenmaier's heavy uneven steps thump along the hallway into the bathroom. He is clearing his throat, loosening stuff off the bottom of his stomach and spitting it into the sink, a big glob from the sound of it. Then I hear him pee and flush before limping back. 'I love my limp,' he told me once, 'it saved my life when I was in Stalingrad in Russia. A bomb exploded not too close and not too far from me. They airlifted me back to Germany just before the long deadly battle. The other two million were not so lucky.'

Frau Rittenmaier is next, fresh out of bed. She smells deliciously yeasty like a fresh bun from the bakery. Wrapped into my dry blanket I move the wet mattress out of the little puddle jumper's reach.

"Good morning, Monika." She is using my real name. It doesn't sound right anymore.

"Frau Rittenmaier?"

"What, my dear, tell me."

"I wet my bed." Mortified, I huddle inside the blanket, draw it closely, eyes closed like a little child trying not to exist.

"Oh my, it's just a mattress; and thanks, you already moved it."

What did I expect? A beating with a belt the way it happened long ago whenever I wet my bed?

She goes back to her room and returns with an armful of clothes. I didn't even have to beg. With the help of countless safety pins, she folds and molds everything onto my body, steps back and says: "that'll work just fine." Then she gets herself ready while Herr Rittenmaier sets the table, makes coffee and brings breakfast.

The five of us squeeze into their little alcove. It's amazing what Martina can do sitting on Papa's lap with a little cereal, milk and raisins, and lots of imagination. Her hair, face, hands, clothes, part of the floor and Papa himself turn into a work of art while Josef eats every single crumb, and even his bib stays clean. The show of love, the lack of violence is breathtaking against the cruel emptiness of my life. Or should I embrace this vision, remember it as a guide for my own future life rather than pitying myself all the time?

"Shall I talk to Isabel's Mom today?" I ask Herr Rittenmaier who is about to leave.

"If you do, make sure no other ears are listening."

"Especially no kids' ears," adds Frau Rittenmaier. "We need to find the right people to tell it to." She is helping her husband with his tie, then he puts on his coat and hat, kisses the six rosy cheeks of his family and shakes my hand goodbye.

"I am good at keeping secrets, bad at giving them up. You know that. I have carried them all my life, and they sure weigh a lot."

"Do what you think is right. You have good instincts, Monika," says Frau Rittenmaier. Her praise makes me proud, but I am not ready to be called Monika. "I like the sound, maybe one day it will feel right again."

"I understand. Come back here after school, please."

"After I visit Mother." And off I go. She follows me with bread and butter for lunch, and I cry from happiness and despair all at the same time for so much kindness.

The happenings of the last forty-eight hours are fermenting in my belly. It growls, protesting the toxic brew which is my life. Teachers' voices ring from afar, I have no answers, not even whether I am feeling all right. On my way home with Isabel I suddenly wish she weren't coming. I wish it were my home, my Mother, my piano. The safety pin in Frau Rittenmaier's underwear is rubbing me and hurts. Why didn't she fasten it properly! It irritates me. She irritates me with her little pathetic wisdoms!

As she often does, Frau Dietrich invites me to share their midday meal before I practice the piano. There is red cabbage, steaming hot rice and my favorite sausages. They make me gag and she wonders why I don't like sausages today. I shrug my shoulders. How can I explain? She keeps throwing glances my way, worried, wondering. Does she notice my insides are foaming and frothing, my whole body is fidgety and on edge? I want to suck my hair and twirl it and I want to be angry at somebody or everybody. As soon as we are done eating, she sends Isabel to take Nicholas for a haircut. He just had it cut. It must be an excuse to be alone with me.

"What is happening, Klara, and don't say 'nothing'. Look at me."

I don't but help clear the dishes, say a few words. Just a few.

Then I tell her most of the story, and then it all pours out like an overflowing garbage can, putrid, nauseating, but there is no stopping. Everything that I know and told the Rittenmaiers, the whole dirty laundry, it's all out now. She comes and hugs me for a long time. Her eyes are watery when she looks at me. I tell her that I fear the police. But I don't tell her about Father and how he touched me. It seems too shameful, and how could she understand.

"Oh, my dear, thank you for trusting me. This is a horrible, horrible story, I am so very sorry. Let me call my husband. We finally got a phone. Don't look so worried. He will know what to do. He is a police officer and a good man."

She dials, listens and says "Helmut, do you have a moment?"

I walk away. Playing the piano is what I need now. I grab the keys, play fast and loud and forget all else till Frau Dietrich talks to me.

"Don't go back to your house. My husband knows the right people who will take care of you. Stay here. Isabel and Nicholas will gladly share their room, and Isabel has a few clothes which don't fit her anymore, if you don't mind."

I want to throw my arms around her but freeze. I can finally accept hugs but can't give them yet. Instead I continue to play the piano, even when Isabel and Nicholas are back. Why are they back? I don't really like them. Suddenly they are part of what's wrong with my life.

When night is about to fall, I bike to the hospital. Night does not fall I think, it gently dances its slow dance with the day. Only people fall on us and hurt us with their hate.

. . .

Mother is better. She is awake and looks at me with her dark beady eyes. I sit down, take her hand in mine and she does not resist.

"You are better, I hear."

"I might have another stroke, a worse one. If it happens, I don't want to live, remember that." She talks slowly, garbles her sounds and it is hard to understand. Drool is running down on one side of her mouth.

"Tell that to Father. If you want to be dead, he'll gladly kill you. He tried killing me yesterday, or something, I can't be sure. I ran away and won't be back, ever."

She is looking at me intensely, a flicker of life in her eyes. Something is on her mind. Then she speaks to me like she never did before.

"I need to tell you things. It's time. He killed my baby, didn't want it, and he killed his own brother whom I loved. They were twins and looked somewhat alike. With the war going on nobody knew who was who, and which one came back from the war. He buried him in the back yard next to my baby where the soil is soft, and nobody hears the cries of the dead."

I am too stunned to speak or move. We simply stare at each other for a long time. I keep holding her hand and hope she won't die before telling me all she knows. I would like her to die, however, right afterwards.

"Your Mother screamed 'Kurt', as soon as I snatched you. She was hurt and bleeding and had another young one close by. I guess Kurt might have been your Father, if you ever want to search."

The nurse brings her some medicine and checks her blood pressure.

"Your blood pressure is too high," she says. "Your visitor needs to go."

Mother shakes her head. "I need another moment." Then she rests again for a while. Drools a bit more.

"I was never married. Hans, the real butcher, was the love of my life. He picked me off the road and took me to the house. He saved my life. We fell in love."

"Why didn't you leave after he murdered them? Why didn't you leave years ago?"

"Ach. The shock and such fear. The war was still raging, and I was Jewish. Still am. Later, I was in denial. Couldn't handle life. Never turned him in from fear he'd still get me from the grave or from prison. By then, there was too much dirt on me, too. Nothing more to say." She turns her head and I know she is finished.

There are so many more questions. She had a baby. Father killed it. He tried to kill me too, or did he? I can't wrap my brain around any of it. Why would she have stayed? Did she ever love him, the mean, smelly son of a bitch? Was he ever kind and gentle?

I leave the hospital, heavy with thoughts and tired from listening to her garbled and slurred sounds, watching her slow drool drip over her chin. No, I don't think he ever was a kind-hearted human being. He was born a sleaze ball, a degenerate perverted scumbag with a rotten heart, and a fucking murderer. How many people did he kill? It's dark outside, empty and bitter cold. I take my bike and pedal towards the Rittenmaiers. A car has been following me for a while it seems. I turn my head, it's too dark to see and I get paranoid, drive around randomly and in circles. It follows me around every corner, close behind, the bright lights glaring. In front of a house people are talking with the door open. I jump off the bike and run towards them. The car drives on, but I can hear it turn around. I veer into bushes and into the neighbor's yard and beyond, take cover behind sheds and under trees, listen to every sound, avoid street lights and make it to the Rittenmaiers just as a car comes slowly driving by, its high beams glaring across the road and partly into their yard. It stops. They are still trying to find me. Not many people in town own a car, and I am sure it is the same one. I run, my back bent low, into the side yard deep into the shadows of an evergreen and crawl under its wet gnarly branches spreading out low and far over the cold ground. It is a good shelter and I hold still, my head down, my hands curled into fists, my heart beating so loud it might burst and give me away.

The car door opens and closes again. A man walks towards the front door, tall and very thin like a lamppost, his tiny head barely visible under a large hat. He puts on tinted glasses with a big dark frame, then rings the bell. Frau Rittenmaier opens the door as he steps back into the shadows, pulling his hat even further down the way Father does.

"Sorry to bother you." He clicks his heels together. "Is there a young girl in your house, or do you expect one?" His voice is scratchy, and he mumbles; hard to understand.

"Sorry. Do I know you?" The man stays in the dark.

"No. Thanks for your help." He tips his hat with his finger, bows his head, then clicks his heels again and leaves. He drives off but I stay put, don't trust him; and after a few minutes, he slowly drives around again and stops just past their gate. I hear his footsteps. He comes into the yard and quietly looks around bushes and trees. I squeeze as close to the ground as I can and hold my breath. He is coming, his flashlight shining just about close enough to discover me. I close my eyes into a squint, maybe he won't see me then, when a noise in the next tree makes him move over and shine his flashlight into it. A squirrel, that's all. A squirrel saved my life. Now he starts peeking into windows. The curtains are wide open, and he walks around the whole house. Then he leaves again. Not till the engine is on and the car drives off do I take a deep breath and uncurl my fists, feel the wetness from lying on the cold ground. After several more minutes I get up and walk to the back door. There is no light to give me away, and I give it a loud knock. Frau Rittenmaier comes and opens it slightly. I put my finger over my mouth before she opens hers.

"Psssst. Don't let the kids see me. Close the curtains, all of them." She looks taken aback but does what I asked. I stay outside till she lets me in.

"You look terrified. A guy was looking for you, I believe."

"I lay squeezed and twisted under your large tree. It hurt. A car was following me; he looked like a scarecrow is all I could see."

"Goodness me. Goodness gracious. Stay here in our bedroom, keep the door closed."

I slump onto their bed, a pitiful bundle of pain from the cold, the wet and the fear, my face and hands scratched and bleeding. It is out of my hands now. What did the car look like? Like all cars at night, dark with a rattle. Blood is running down my forehead. I get up before it messes up their linens and go into the bathroom to clean up.

When Herr Rittenmaier comes home, I watch them feed the kids and get them to bed early. She sings a good night song with her high voice, clear as a protestant church bell while he adds beautiful low harmonies. His voice is mellow, rich with the flavor of Frau Dietrich's chocolate pudding. Then they whisper, make phone calls with quiet, hurried voices. There is food in the kitchen. I am starving but can't eat. My nerves are on fire from Mother's words and being followed and I can't sit still, twirl and suck my hair till it is twisted into a slimy wet noodle, the way I used to do a long time ago.

"Isabel's Father will pick you up in a while," he says, joining me at the table while she is silently wiping off the blood from my scratches. My legs jerk with a nervous twitch and I sigh, balling my hands into fists again. I tell them about what Mother said. Everything, it all needs to come out before my insides rot from the muck.

By the time I am done telling, Isabel's Father is at the door. I don't know him and feel shy, but one look at him, and I smile back. He is like Nicholas in big, a freckled face under reddish curls and a mischievous glint in his eyes. He is tall and slender with strong shoulders and stretches out his long arm for a handshake.

"I am Herr Dietrich. You must be Klara. I bet you could use a long warm bath." He shakes my hand with a most dazzling smile as if the world were a great place. I curtsey and tell him I have an idea. They all look at me, surprised. So am I. Didn't know I had any ideas at all.

"I jumped off my bike at a house not far from here. People were saying goodbye at the front door. I ran towards them for help, then heard the car turn around and ran away in panic. Maybe whoever followed me went to that house. Maybe those people knew him. It's a small town."

Frau Rittenmaier and I feel badly that our only description of him is of a lamppost or a scarecrow.

"Not to worry," he says, "you are a clever girl, Klara. Let's go stop by that house right now."

It's the last thing I want to do, and I pull away.

"Klara, bad guys fear me. They hide and pray. We are the scary ones; just look at us."

We both laugh, we so do not look scary, and I leave feeling safe just because.

He takes me by my arm and walks me to his car, an old beat up VW.

The cold is coming down hard and heavy, wrapping around me like Father did. There won't be any snow tonight with such cold. The air is filled with the smoke of fires. I show him which house it was, and he parks in front. We go to the door and he knocks. A strong knock. He is the police and won't pussyfoot around. I stay close to him just in case. A lady with a mop of short blonde curls and bouncy breasts opens the door, her face turning into an instant smile.

"Helmut, what a surprise. Come on in, how are you?"

11

ENTER HERR ROSEN

We sit down in her living room. Her husband sits by her side, bald and barely noticeable but for his little snores. His book is about to fall off his lap.

"We won't be long, Sofie. Tell me, did somebody come within the last hour and a half to ask about a girl?"

"Yes, it was the police chief's assistant. He thought somebody was robbing a house. He was quite agitated, wanted to make sure we were all right."

"What did he look like?"

"Tall and very skinny. We laughed because he looked like our lamppost. We never saw him before and couldn't really see his face under the hat."

Herr Dietrich thanks her, and we get up; asks if her back is getting better.

"Not really. I might have to get used to it."

"Take it easy, Sofie. Don't let her work too hard," he yells, turning to her husband whose book has dropped and whose snores would do a walrus proud.

. . .

Silently we drive up and down small hills through town and out of town, through the next town and out of that one and further yet. Never have I been halfway that far, and I wish I could see through the dark night what the world looks like. We finally stop at a large two-story house lit up with plenty of lights, its curtains closed. We walk up a nicely paved walkway past two lit lanterns as if we were expected. Somebody is playing the piano.

A dark-haired man in his thirties or beyond opens the door. We quickly enter and close it against the frigid air.

"Good evening, Herr Rosen, thanks for staying up."

"Good evening, Herr Dietrich. And you must be Klara." His very dark eyes radiate with a strong energy that pierces me like a dagger. We shake hands, and I curtsey. Nobody says any unnecessary words. There is an almost sacred importance in this moment, and I must try to remember it, this fork in my life; if it truly is a fork and not another knife in my heart. We take off our shoes and follow him into a large living room. The men sink into big brown easy chairs that make them look like boys. Herr Rosen points to a sofa for me to sit on, and I lean into its flowery cushions. I don't hear any more piano playing, but somebody is ransacking the kitchen.

"Uta, we are ready," he calls. There follows the sound of liquid being poured, and I give it a look around. It is a warm home and elegant like Herr Rosen, and it is alive with a newspaper on the coffee table, one slipper kicked off earlier than the other near the fireplace. There is a book waiting to be read and a fern that needs watering. A carpeted staircase leads to the upstairs. Once again, I realize that the mess in our house is old and has a smell, it crouches in corners, hides on top of cupboards and inside its drawers. Our mess is an enemy; theirs is a friend.

"Hello, Klara." A familiar voice in a blue bathrobe is walking towards us with a tray and four cups of tea. "Haven't seen you since at least Wednesday."

"Frau Graf!" I get up to curtsey, and she puts down the tray and grabs me for an insanely intense hug.

"I had to learn everything about you from other people, you naughty girl! I am sorry you couldn't trust me enough. I can get scary at times, I know!"

Herr Rosen lifts his cup to his lips. The hot liquid startles him and spills into the saucer and onto his pullover, and he wipes it carefully with his handkerchief. What a handsome man he is with his black hair cropped short, its dark color in stark contrast to pearly white teeth and cold rimmed glasses. His is a look of intelligence and importance. He is looking at me now, his eyes peering deep into mine.

"Klara, you are going to stay here for a while. Stay inside the house, don't go near windows, and don't open the door to anybody. You are safe, but I don't want rumors that a young girl is staying here, not while somebody is looking for you. There are lots of books you can read and plenty of food. I work in this town, and we have a phone should you need anything. Frau Graf is my good friend. We have known each other for a long time."

He looks at her, and their eyes lock.

"It's been an epic voyage." Her voice is quiet and meant only for him. I feel like an intruder, realizing they are sweethearts.

. . .

"What will happen to Mother? She will be released today. He won't pick her up."

"Then she'll have to stay another day; don't worry about her."

"Please, can you tell me what's going on? What you think Father did, just anything you know, please?"

"I am mainly working on finding specific war criminals, you know, Nazis who have committed crimes against humanity on a large scale. If what you said is correct about your Father, we might have a good chance to catch one of those, but we must be careful. There are plenty of people fighting those of us who try to find them. Ach." And with one deep breath, he rolls his shoulders, lifts his arms and scrunches his nose. He has a most beautiful voice, like the lower part of a piano,

and very gentle. Even better than Herr Rittenmaier.

"You could be an opera singer," I say, and he laughs and shakes his head.

"I could not but thank you."

"He could, but he'd get all the notes wrong," explains Frau Graf. "Let's go to bed, and you, Herr Dietrich, go home to your wife and kids. Sleep well."

Yes, Frau Graf is a bit bossy, but she gets to the point, and he leaves. I get my own little room, a bed made up with nice sheets, maybe even freshly laundered. They sure smell good. Mine have never been washed that I know of since I stopped peeing in bed. I rest my head on the fluffy pillow and start looking at the picture right above the wall, there is red and yellow, maybe green. The colors blend into one, and a deep sleep takes me far away till early morning, when I wake up gasping for air. I was naked and someone tried to suffocate me.

It was Father. I shove him away, get up and act especially
cheerful to spite him.

12

HIGH ABOVE A LAKE

"Good Morning, Frau Graf, you are still around and in your robe." My smile is feverish and fake, and my toothy grin feels malevolent. Father is still inhabiting me.

"I decided to stay here with you. We can have us some nice talks. I already got fresh little buns from the bakery. No, not in my robe, don't look so disgusted. Or is that a smile? Girl, what happened to you? Did you have nightmares? Let me make you some tea."

"Coffee is fine. That's all I ever had."

She shakes her head in judgment of my early coffee drinking. "Bad. But we are all lucky just to be alive, you know. Let's not forget that. You are a strong girl, and you will be stronger for having overcome so many obstacles."

We sit in a cozy corner at a small round table with the sun's first rays shining through the light curtains, and we gently hug our coffee cups with both hands for the warmth.

"Why do you say we are all so lucky to be alive?"

"Our little towns around here were fairly safe during the war. Nobody wanted to waste their bombs on us. Not so in the big cities. You never saw their utter devastation, have you? You were too young. Black ruins and well-fed rats feeding off the dead, not much else. Now it's much better."

"On photos only. I couldn't really tell."

"We'll take you to the big city one day. You'll see what wars do to people or rather what people do to people. And don't forget the hundreds of thousands of mines on the ground. Everywhere. They will keep killing for years to come."

I remember that the cousin of a boy from school just lost his leg to a mine, and a girl in the next town died a year ago. I never truly understood what it meant till now. I guess the closer to us things happen the more they matter.

"How do you know Herr Rosen?"

"It's a long story. Let's enjoy our coffee in peace. Then I'll get dressed and, no offense my dear friend, you must take a bath before we sit down for a second cup and buttered buns with jam or honey."

"I have never had a bath. All I have is a pitcher of water in my room and a washcloth. Do you think I am smelly at times? You should smell my Father. Mother says: 'like a fox fart through a goat's ass.'

"Stop it! I'll make sure to stay away from him. Girl! do not describe people that way. You and I know that he is a pile of shit, sorry, but in company you simply say he smells bad, or, to be fancy, you could call him a bit odoriferous."

"I am trying. Mother swears and talks like that all day long, and he is worse."

"We are all animals and get a bit smelly, don't you worry. But use gentle words."

. . .

She turns the hot water on for me and fills the tub, then leaves
to get dressed. I lower myself, naked, into this delicious water
which covers me to above my breasts. I feel suspended, feel my
body getting limp and heavy, my mind light and empty, on the
verge of something beautiful like falling asleep and drowning.
What a way to go; an end, a new beginning. Who knows. Who
cares. Wait and see. I slowly slide down the rounded backside
of the tub. Gravity is gentle, and not till water enters my nose
does my body react with a powerful jolt. I sneeze and cough,
and the rage is coming back. I stare at the curly hair of my bush
and feel exposed. It is way too easy to get to. Skirts don't
protect. It could happen again; anybody stronger than I am can
easily go there. 'Good girl,' he called me, 'good girl,' and his
voice brings back the terror and the smell and the images of you
know what. What did he really do to me? Squeeze his private
parts against me and get me wet. Could that be how to make a
baby?

The hot water turns cold far too quickly. I get out and dress. If I
ever truly wanted to kill myself, it would be in the gentleness of
water. But it's not what I want. I want to take more of these
baths. One day I shall have my own and bathe with a book in
my hands for hours. No. I could never kill myself. I'd rather kill
him because he deserves it; I don't. And I like boys. Or do I? An
attack of bile rises from my stomach and makes me nauseous.

"Did you use soap and shampoo?" Frau Graf is back.

"No, I think not." I am cheerful again and laugh out loud at
nothing. How easy it is to turn feelings inside out and bottom
up like Father wanted; laugh away the pain.

"I thought so. There is no ring around the tub. Tomorrow

morning you'll take another bath, and I'll help scrub you. No discussion."

What's a ring around the tub? I wonder.

What's so funny, wonders Frau Graf.

We go downstairs and eat in silence. The buns are fresh and delicious, and the coffee tastes better than any I've ever had in my life. But I barely eat or drink. Don't have the stomach for it. Then we go to the sofa and sit down, one on each end.

"I like to put my legs up," she says and stretches out her well-shaped legs. Her varicose vein crawls inside her left leg like a snake, the kind that suffocates its prey, and I shiver.

"Girl, you are pale as a ghost! You are trembling. A moment ago, you laughed for no reason."

"Your story will help take my mind off the bastard."

"Well then, let me tell you how I met Herr Rosen." And she begins her tale.

"It happened on the outer ledge of a rock high above a deep lake. I was the only person in the world, at least for many kilometers in each direction. I was 20 years old and distressed in such a deep way by what was happening in Germany that I got stomach ulcers, got sleep deprived from nightmares and suffered debilitating headaches. I had enrolled at the University of Freiburg but could barely manage. Friends of mine disappeared with their entire families. Neighbors were taken at night. I heard the screams. My favorite aunt was euthanized in a hospital where she had gone for depression. Simple depression. And here I was, struck by the horror and feeling both relief and guilt. Relief for not being Jewish, guilt that I could survive simply by not being Jewish.

So here I sat on this ledge on a rock and started to scream from the top of my lungs, screamed to the birds, to the wind and the clouds, over the cliff to the black water deep below. I wanted to scream it to the world. Slowly, my screams turned into song. Random songs, popular songs, then beautiful art songs and arias to let the world know what man can do besides bring war and death. All the beauty that makes us great and happy and thoughtful, I sang it on that rock.

When I stopped, exhausted from the screams, shivering from the cold and the raw emotions rushing through my veins, I held still. There was a sound, not from an animal I thought.

"Anybody there? Yoohoo!" I called out loud, a bit uneasy alone on this high ledge.

"It's just me, David. Helloooo! Are you feeling better?"

"And this handsome dark-haired guy poked his head around the corner, grinning from ear to ear. Oh, what a grin. And what a voice. Soothing, mellow, and large. And that's how we fell in love, on the ledge of a rock high above a lake. That was a long time ago," she muses.

"Did you kiss?"

"Maybe. Maybe not. None of your business. I fell off the ledge and nearly drowned. He jumped after me and saved my life."

"And then you kissed him?"

"He blew air into my mouth to resuscitate me, yes, if you call that a kiss then we kissed. Let's take a break now. We can sit and read a book for a while." She takes a book but never turns the page. Her eyes are staring into the past while I try to find memories for the future, for my future.

The telephone rings. She picks it up, pushes it hard against her ear. Her eyes light up, and her voice rises an octave. She must be talking to Herr Rosen, all sweet and honey. Then she hangs up and tells me the newest news.

"They took the chief of police and his assistant in for questioning. Apparently, there have been lingering suspicions regarding their history during the war. Let's go to your house and pick up your stuff."

"I'll never want to go in that house again."

"Then let's visit your Mother. I'll follow you around like a puppy dog. You'll be so safe you'll hate it."

That sounds agreeable. We leave and this time I see the landscape whizz by in the daylight hours. It's a peaceful countryside with small towns and farms clinging to hillsides and nestled in valleys. No signs of any damage from the war. I am surprised how many churches there are. Every small village has a catholic and a protestant church like they can't get along with each other under one roof. Isn't it supposed to be one God?

"Do you go to church, Frau Graf?"

"Never. The church has done nothing for me. If there is a God, he will understand. We have fascinating conversations, the two of us. I have yelled at him more than once."

"Yelled and given advice!" I say, and she giggles like a young girl.

13

TWO BAD GUYS

Mother's bed is empty. A nurse tells us a big heavy man picked her up against doctor's orders.

"Sounds like Father."

"She must be back at your house. Let's go check on her."

"I hate this wicked woman. I owe her nothing."

"You don't owe her. But you are a good person who cares about living things like rats and cockroaches and even your Mother."

"I don't like that he was going to let her die on the floor, is all."

We drive back to Frau Graf's house. Frau Rittenmaier calls to let me know she washed my wet clothes and found quite a bit of cash in one of my pockets.

"I stole it from our cash register. Believe me, it is hard earned money! See you in a minute."

She is waiting at the door to keep me quiet since the twins are napping. We quickly shake hands. Then she hands me my money and I pick up my bike from the night before and leave for my first shopping trip ever. It feels powerful. I choose, I pay, and I own. Two pairs of underwear later, plus two pairs of long brown stockings with a pattern, a fuzzy green sweater and a pleated skirt, I return to Frau Graf and throw my new treasures onto her sofa. She lets me skip the rest of the school day since two policemen were at our house. In a small town, rumors grow from a seed into a frenzy of gossip. I could not handle it today. All I want is another bath, wash off the filth from my life as a butcher's daughter and the feel of his sickening hands on me. One bath was not enough! A hundred might not be enough.

"I expect a student in a few minutes. Eat if you are hungry and empty your bladder. Don't bother us during the lesson."

Ach, such a bossy lady! How I love her. She is unaware that she unleashed my inner Rottweiler into action during Father's attack and saved my life. One day, I will thank her for it.

Her lesson over, the student gone, we go back to Herr Rosen's house in the other town. She has a key to his house, and we go straight to the kitchen and the small pantry. There are salad makings, bread and butter, Swiss cheese and liverwurst, Sauerkraut and sausages. I take everything out except for the sausages. Just thinking about them makes my bile come up. He comes home shortly after us. They kiss, and I come close to watch, stretch my neck a bit to see better.

"What are you gawking at?" She stares at me, then grabs him and kisses him again with all she's got, and he quite likes it, and they are stuck by their lips and kiss and kiss. When they fall apart, laughing, he says:

"That show was just for you."

I guess my smile is spread all over my face from watching

them. It feels important to see touches that come from love, more now than ever.

"Gross," I say with immense pleasure, and break into a freaky loud laugh, bizarre, irrational and ludicrous. I can't help it, and they stare at me but say nothing.

Quietly we finish making an early dinner together. I set the table, he slices the bread, a very dark and hard bread with a sweet and nutty taste. The longer you chew the better it tastes. The salad is done, and we sit down to eat.

"Olives," she says, offering me a small bowl with little round green things. They are new to me and no, I don't like them but eat a couple to be polite.

"Look at your face, girl. Don't waste them on yourself, please, unless you love them."

I admire her candidness. I don't have to eat them, and she'll get more. Life can be so simple.

After dinner, Frau Graf makes a fresh pot of coffee. We slowly drink it, trying to stretch out the short time of pleasure. Neither one of them even bothers to look at today's headlines. Soon enough, he'll have things to tell us, I am sure. He takes off his gold rimmed glasses, cleans them with a fresh handkerchief then blows his nose in it before putting them back on. He is ready.

"So, we picked up those two guys today. They didn't seem surprised. I guess, Klara, with your Mother in the hospital and you moving out of the house that night, the scarecrow went looking for you. Your Father must have mentioned that you have dirt on them and know their secret, whatever it is. By the way, Klara, I still don't understand what he had in mind squeezing you so hard. People don't kill that way. Frankly,

Klara, I don't buy it. It makes no sense. Tell what happened to Frau Graf when you are ready. Understood?"

His dark shiny eyes rest on me. I blush and turn my head, stare into a corner, mortified. He sees through me and knows what might have happened. Then he continues.

"The police chief has a lot of bad history. He worked in the concentration camp near here, but that by itself is not a crime. His assistant is not an assistant at all but a farmhand. An obnoxious fellow, a scarecrow by his looks, you got that right, but even dumber. All he said was Father brings them free meat, and then they drink to it. We let him go for now. Ach!"

Frau Graf refills his cup of coffee, then kisses the top of his head. He takes a sip and continues.

"We kept the police chief in custody. He smells of something bad besides his underwear. Ach. Unfortunately, it takes a long time to find out the truth about so many things. Too much paperwork was burned in the war, and too many witnesses were killed. He lives alone, says he came from the Baltic states without any paperwork. We are circulating his photos in all of the police stations in Germany now."

"That will take weeks! And how about Father's photo?"

"We must first find out which brother he really is. Who killed whom?"

"Mother will know. We need to get her out of the house, but I doubt she'll talk at the police station. She'll be too nervous."

Frau Graf suggests we bring Mother to her place in the morning around ten. "That will give us enough time for a good scrub in the bathtub."

"How will we get her out of the house?" I worry. "Father won't hesitate to use his meat cleaver."

"We'll figure it out. We are the police. We love crazy dangerous people." Herr Rosen winks at me with a twinkle in his eyes, the way Herr Dietrich did to make me feel safe. It's hard to be scared when either one of them is around. He speaks with authority, and the calmness of his voice tastes like Frau Graf's coffee, deep, strong and rich with cream which I have gotten to love. And he wears such fancy suits with a handkerchief in its breast pocket. Why does he not wear a uniform, I wonder out loud?

"I am a special investigator with the police. A detective. Don't worry. I can shoot and put you away in handcuffs if needed."

We are exhausted from the day, its many emotions and unanswered questions. I forget about the rest of their love story. There is no space left in my brain.

"Good night! See you tomorrow around the bathtub," I say and go upstairs to sleep.

"Can't wait to use soap and show you the ring," she calls after me.

14

MORE ABOUT MOTHER

After an intense scrubbing by Frau Graf, everywhere but where she told me to do my own scrubbing, I check my skin. There shouldn't be any left, instead it feels prickly and alive.

"Frau Graf. I feel clean enough for the next decade. You could make money scrubbing people or floors. Or people on floors."

"Girl, are you trying to be funny? This was to teach you how to wash and smell clean every day, unless you want people to stay away from you."

Deeply embarrassed, -I probably always stink - I stare at the color of the bath water, which is not at all the color of water, and as it goes down the drain a wide black ring is forming around the tub. That's what the ring is, my dirt come to life like a second coming, like Jesus. She barely lets me get dressed before handing me a rag and cleaning powder.

"Get to work, girl."

And I scrub the dirt off the tub. It doesn't seem right to have

to scrub it twice, first off my body, then off the tub. It dimin-
ishes the pleasure of bathing.

"Sit. Now tell me about the scars on your body. They can't
possibly all be from accidents."

"I didn't know I had many scars. I have never seen them.
They happened long ago during the first few years. Later, I
only got beatings, hit over the head or in the face. Lots of nose
bleeds in those days!"

"You have four large scars, many little ones or cuts, and
burn marks."

"Oh yes. Father used his butcher tools. Mother added the
burns. Those hurt more than the cuts, I remember. They never
smoked but she had some cigarettes."

"Ach, such a cruel world. I would hug you, but you are too
naked."

At about nine o'clock we leave and drive to her apartment. She
has no students in the morning, and she and I put a sheet on the
sofa for Mother to stretch out.

"It's to keep her smell from my sofa, not for her comfort."

We pull up chairs for the police and me to sit on, then she
goes to the kitchen and puts the coffee on, and that's all.

At 9:45, Herr Rosen comes by in an unmarked police car
with two young, tough looking officers. There will be room in it
to bring Mother. Another three officers will join us at the
butchery to deal with Father.

For the moment, my fear of Father is gone knowing that six
officers will be there. Father will most likely act like a coward.
But there is a great anxiety in me, a furor and confusion. What

will happen when I see him? The blubbery ball of shit who touched my breasts, whispered 'good girl' and rubbed my belly with filth on his hands. Sent an electric shock wave down my spine. I want to see the wound left by my bite, hope it got infected from the hate I felt in my teeth. I can't hold still, ball and unball my hands and start to twitch my nose the way Herr Rosen likes to do.

"Hey, one nose is enough. If you must twitch find your own body part, girl."

I give Frau Graf the evil eye! Did she have to say it out loud?"

We leave at 9:55 and arrive at the house minutes later. Another half a minute and the other car joins us. I tell them that his truck is gone, and he won't be there, which they don't seem to mind, and neither do I.

Mother doesn't answer, is probably still too sick, and I get the key from under the doormat and open the door, forgetting all about hiding behind Herr Rosen as I run through the kitchen.

"Mother!" All is quiet. I go to the bedroom and slowly open the door. The room smells so horribly rotten I can't get myself to describe it. I thought I knew all of life's smells, but it stinks worse than it ever has, and I don't want to use my worst words in front of Herr Rosen. I can barely stand to breathe. She is in bed looking like a corpse again.

"Mother." I sit down next to her. She moves her hand, and I take it.

"Go. Go now. He is trying to find you. He will kill you."

Why is she worried about me, the old hag? Why now?

"We need to get you out of this shithole before you die from the stench."

"If he kills me, I am ready for it."

"I am not, God damnit." I call Herr Rosen who comes in and stops at the door. He can't breathe either.

"Father is out trying to kill me," I say, "we better get going."

He calls to the two strong guys, waves them in and they, too, stop at the door from the sudden assault on their noses. Then they lift and drag and carry Mother to the car and put her in the back, their noses held to the side throughout, trying not to breathe. I quickly run upstairs into my little room to get my clothes and stare at that frightful metal hook on the wall. All these years, a butcher's hook meant for a large carcass. Why did I never pull it out?

Through the window, I see a truck way back in the yard but forget about it as soon as I am back at the car. There is too much on my mind.

It is as if mother gave up on life. A helpless old woman with no struggles left. Her head is leaning against me, and she doesn't mind when the two officers take her upstairs into Frau Graf's apartment and gently lift her onto the sofa. She is so still and small. How was I ever scared of her? I put a pillow under her head and ask if she is warm enough. All she does is look at me and shake her head ever so slightly 'no'. Herr Rosen brings her a blanket.

"Would you like some coffee?" She nods.

"Do you want food?" She nods again.

Frau Graf pours coffee, and I hold the cup. Slowly she sips, then again and again. Then I feed her some lentil soup. She takes a bite of that, too, and then she stops.

"You want me to talk while I still can?" She says in her raspy slurry voice that is almost not of this world any longer.

"That's why we are here," replies Herr Rosen, "I want to

make sure you are warm enough. And please stop when you get tired. We will take care of you and find your husband. That's my job. I am a detective."

It is the first time in all my years with her that she does not look frightened or particularly mean. Did her meanness stem from fear that Father might kill her? All these years? No courage ever to go for help, be a normal person? It is so sad, but she did steal me, the old bitch.

Herr Rosen sits down close to Mother. I move a bit further down; still don't like her, this wicked woman, but I care enough to hold her hand with some compassion and with the hope of finding answers.

"What is your name?" asks Herr Rosen.

"That was a long time ago," she begins, "and no, he is not my husband, the bastard. I am from Berlin, Rachael Kohn is my name. Yes, Jewish and I was very pretty. Promising, people said. Petrified by fear all my life. Several gestapo officers raped me one night. They left me to die on the snow at the side of the road in the middle of winter. A car picked me up shortly after and a man took me home. This was his home, the butchery. Hans was a lovely man, kind and caring, and we fell in love. He did not mind when I realized I was with child from the rape.

"Don't worry," he said, "I'll be the child's father. Let's get married when the war is over, and you won't have to hide." He knew I was Jewish.

"He had a twin, an identical twin, Fritz. He worked at the concentration camp and would sometimes come visit on weekends. A nasty guy, and we didn't like when he came. He seemed jealous of our happiness and of the fact that the store

was his brother's and not his. He was enraged that I was pregnant with a child that would not be of his family. When the
baby was born, he never tried to bond with her.

"One fateful day a couple of years later, I will never
forget....., a very strong wind was howling all day, bending many
trees and breaking them like match sticks. We lost half of our
orchard, we feared for the roof on the house, and the child was
screaming, when Fritz suddenly grabbed her from my arms
with the look in his eyes of a truly crazed person. He went
berserk. He killed her right in front of me, barely three years
old at the time. Took her and broke her neck as if she were a
chicken for the next meal. He took her along in his arm, the
only time he carried her, then killed my beloved Hans with his
meat cleaver. I wished he had killed me. I wanted to die but
couldn't do it. Didn't have the guts, I guess. Couldn't leave
either. The war was not over by then, and I was still Jewish."

She stops, as exhausted from talking with her numb cheek as
we are trying to understand her slurred speech. I feed her a bit
more coffee and soup, and she continues her story. How
anxious she seems to tell it, get it off her chest.

"Something of me died that day. Most of me died, I guess.
He moved in, took over the store and me. Raped me, and I
couldn't leave. Couldn't make decisions. Then he wanted a
family, but I produced no more offspring.

She shudders with a deep sob, pulls the blanket a bit closer
to her chin, her eyes sunken beads in her sparrow like face.

"So, he knew you were Jewish?" asks Herr Rosen.

"Yes. He didn't mind at all. He said: 'Jewish girls sure are
pretty.' One day, on a whim, I took off to go back to Berlin, see
if anybody from my family was alive, and I came upon thousands of people fleeing the Russians. I heard that the war was

about to end. I hadn't planned on stealing a child. It was just, when I saw you, looking like my baby did at that age, I grabbed you and ran. You were my baby, mine. I've always regretted it because we couldn't bond. Me with my broken mind, you with your smarts, you always knew I was an impostor. I won't apologize. There is no forgiving for what I did. I never even checked on my family. If there were survivors, I doubt they would want to meet me after what I've done and what I've become."

She speaks slowly, a bit of spittle pooling in the wrinkles of her droopy cheek, and her eyes bore into the distance of time. She never looks at me or Herr Rosen.

"When I came back with you in my arms, he was livid, a wild animal fuming at the mouth and ready to kill us both. He was so red in the face I prayed for his heart to give up. I told him I would stick around but he was never to touch me again. Then I convinced him that you and I gave him some legitimacy being the butcher in case there were questions. He did not exactly look like his brother, and people had gotten to know my face. They knew there were three people in the house. I became part of the conspiracy and am guilty with whatever you charge me with, officer."

"Did he mention somebody particularly cruel, known as the monster of the camp? Or could Fritz have been the one?" asks Herr Rosen.

"I don't believe so. He would tell stories, horrible stories, and I didn't want to hear them. He did talk about those that found pleasure in torture, enjoyed the screams from... ach, maybe from my own family." She takes a deep breath and sobs but continues as if driven by fear of dying before releasing all she held in for so long. "He did not like it. It was too much even for him. And yes, he mentioned a skinny, tall guy, bald and dumb. I don't know his name, but he was from around here. A laborer of some sort. A sadistic monster he called him, being a monster himself. That tells you something. After he killed my child and Hans, we barely ever talked about anything but some basics. And then we did not talk but yelled and screamed."

Mother must have been starving. She is opening her mouth for more. But she keeps on talking. Herr Rosen has a few more questions about the two friends that Father visits every week.

"Has he ever mentioned anything about them? When he comes back drunk?"

"No. He brings them meat. Quite a good amount."

"Thank you, Frau Fleischer. That will be enough for today. Maybe you can spend the night here until we figure something out for you. And if you remember anything else that might be important, please, please tell us."

Frau Graf comes storming out of her bedroom. "You must be the wicked woman, and I do not like you. I don't want her to spend the night here with me," she says, turning to Herr Rosen. "That woman must go."

I jump up. "Oh, my goodness. I forgot to mention, when I picked up my clothes at the house, I saw a truck way in the back yard. I have never seen any cars back there before. Trucks come only to the butchery to bring animals. He must have been in the house."

"Thanks for telling me. We'll check on him later," says

Herr Rosen. His nose twitches, and he sniffs as if expecting a wretched scene ahead of us. But first he sends his police officers on a search for the tall, skinny guy. "Try the local farms. Be careful, we are dealing with a psychopath."

Then he leaves to question the police chief again.

15

THE BUTCHER ON THE HOOK

"I was a police officer in Berlin." The chief seems nervous under Herr Rosen's pointed glare. "I got greedy, stole expensive items from houses taken by the Gestapo, the secret police. For punishment, they sent me as a guard to a concentration camp. That's where I met 'The Monster.' He was a monster, I was almost scared of him myself, but then we hatched this plan after the war was over to blackmail the fake butcher, Fritz. The Monster knew that Fritz had an identical twin, his name was Hans, who was the actual butcher. I guess Hans died a mysterious death and Fritz took over the store, the name and the woman. We were going to have free meat for the rest of our lives. And that's all I did."

"Are you willing to testify against him?" asks Herr Rosen.

"Yes, and yes again. I am glad you found out before he killed the girl."

"He is still running loose. If he kills her, you will be just as guilty. As a police officer or a human being, you had a duty to turn him in."

And he leaves him in lock-up for now. For his own protection and because he can't stand him.

When Herr Rosen returns to us three ladies, Mother is playing corpse again, I am playing the piano, and Frau Graf is reheating the lentil soup. She is adding some extra celery and carrots to make it last for dinner, and occasionally she yells 'wrong note, wrong note, and I yell back 'I know, I know'. For some reason, I would love it if Mother mentioned my piano playing, gave me some praise. Anything. After all these years, I am still disappointed.

He goes to the kitchen where they hug and whisper. I want to know what's going on and join them.

"Go back, you played so nicely."

"Did not, and what are you talking about? Tell me, it's my life too."

"She must be going through the terrible twos," sighs Frau Graf, "do you seriously consider having kids one day, Herr Rosen?"

"Two girls, two boys and a dog. You know that." He smiles and removes her arms to stir and sniff the soup. He is ready to take Mother back to her house along with an officer for protection. Tomorrow he'll check for a better solution, maybe a hospital bed in a prison.

I try to feed Mother a few more spoons of soup before she leaves, but Frau Graf is too agitated by her presence.

"Take her away. I have a piano student and need to air out the house, it stinks to heaven. How can I charge money?"

Herr Rosen makes a phone call and two young officers show up shortly. They take Mother under her arms and bring her to the police car. Herr Rosen and I take his car. I feel the need to come along, cover her, leave something to drink next to her bed. It's not for her but for me, or who knows. I am not sure of anything.

We get the key from under the mat and open the door while the officers help Mother out of the car. An eerie silence hangs over the house when we enter, more so than this morning. Herr Rosen sniffs.

"It always stinks like death," I tell him. He is not so sure about that, and after putting Mother down on the bed he goes and follows his nose. I chase away one fly, ten flies, twenty that sit listlessly on her wall, then go to bring her some water for the night and a chamber pot. It is too cold and too far for her to go to the outhouse. 'What a nice person I am' is what I think.

"Officer, hurry!" It's Herr Rosen's voice, a shout of dread and foreboding that leaves a hollow echo in the store and forever in my mind. It's as if I know what's waiting there, around the corner in the butchery. I, too, follow the stench, nauseatingly sweet, attracting flies aroused from their winter's sleep. They sit on the blood sausages and liverwurst, on walls and counters without the energy to fly. The putrid stench is unbearable.

"Don't come around the corner," yells Herr Rosen. "Keep her out, officer. And call the coroner for the body to be removed."

I am getting nauseous but feel a powerful pull to peek around that corner. There's a huge thing hanging on a hook, not much different from the usual pieces of meat except for two fat legs dangling down with ugly small swollen feet. Father's feet. It is his corpse, lifeless and black with flies, and a laugh wants to get out, but the puking is coming instead, and I run outside. Herr Rosen follows closely on my heels, barely making it. He wretches miserably and in great volume right next to me, splattering some of the gooey stuff on my shoe and stocking. The officer made his phone call and follows suit. We all look and reek like death. Visions of the huge blubbery fly-covered corpse will follow me for years. But in the midst of this horrible moment lies a relief so powerful, life altering, almost deliciously liberating; the fear is gone, this heavy blanket of concrete I never knew had burdened me most of my life. The rats won't be far behind I hope and eat their share of his flesh. They deserve it. Emptied of all vomit, I go to Mother and tell her Father is dead.

"How?" she asks with a wisp of a voice.

"Looks like he hung himself on a meat hook."

"I don't believe it."

Herr Rosen walks in. "You are right, somebody shot him first and then strung him up. There was lots of blood on his back coming from a head wound. I should say 'sorry for your loss,' but it won't ring true. Good riddance."

"Good riddance," she whispers.

The long nightmare is over. Well, almost. One truly bad guy is still on the run, and Father's evil touch keeps haunting me. When I shoo him away, he comes right back like a pesky fly and sits on my shoulder. He whispers: 'good girl,' into my ear, and the rage comes back, and I feel helpless. I can't even kill him; how can I kill a corpse. One day I'll do what's right when I know what that is.

16

THE PLOT THICKENS

It's been many weeks, with the Monster nowhere in sight. They are searching for him in all areas of the countryside, in empty houses, sheds, in the woods, with no success. He vanished yet I strongly feel his evil presence in the air around us and am sure he is hiding in plain sight despite his height. After all, he could hide as a scarecrow in a farmer's field or as a lamppost in town if he held still. The fear is palpable all over the area since it headlined in the newspaper. Peoples' eyes are keenly aware of what's going on behind trees and corners, behind their backs. More grown men use walking sticks while women carry umbrellas even on sunny days. Everyone is so jumpy that it feeds the fear. Doors get locked, windows closed. Kids are kept off the street.

"Herr Rosen," I tell him, "please check around here. I know he is close."

"We are working on it."

I live with Frau Graf for the time being. Herr Rosen comes every evening and spends the nights to keep us safe. She takes me to school and picks me up. I feel well protected. She would pierce the guy with her stare if he dared to come close, then she'd hit him over the head with her purse so hard he would crumble and ask for mercy. And she would show no mercy but stab him with her umbrella till all his blood ran out.

I do not visit Frau Rittenmaier or Frau Dietrich so as not to endanger them and their families, and I miss them. I only saw Frau Rittenmaier in town once right after it happened.

"You heard, didn't you, that we found Father?"

"Of course, yes, and we are so sorry."

"Pleeease don't be. I am rid of him. Imagine the weight of the bastard off my shoulders."

"I'd rather not. Still, it can't be easy. Please make sure you work through it properly, Klara, don't shrug it off like nothing happened."

"That's what everybody says. They don't know how easy it is. I almost laughed seeing him dead on a hook, but I vomited instead."

"Laughing can be a nervous laugh, a laugh of great relief or sadness, I understand that. It doesn't mean it's a laughing matter. All these years he harmed you, that's what you need to deal with."

I believe she said something important, but it's too much to take in. She is always telling me things. I move on, tired of being told, don't even ask about the kids.

Mother is at a prison hospital about a half hour from here. I have not seen her and barely think about her. And I have not had a single nightmare about Father. But every morning I wake up drenched in cold sweat and gasping for air from being squeezed by 'Big Boy' sausages that come at me from all sides. They smell evil, and their fleshy texture enrages me.

Time passes and people become complacent, stop watching their every step. The Monster must have moved on to where he is not known. I start visiting with the Rittenmaiers and the Dietrichs again. The other day, Herr Rittenmaier asked me to please clean up my dinner plate before leaving.

"It's not my kitchen," I said and watched him do it himself, slowly limping to the kitchen in his hand knitted cardigan. Silly man!

People just don't get me. I am on my own now. Don't want to be told like a child and be what I am not. Let me be me, let me explore and learn what that means. Right now, it's mainly about men and what exactly it is they do with women, and it can't wait. It's like a fire, and I need to let it burn. When a man's eyes are feasting on me, I turn into a rutting cat, want them to play me like a piano, want their fingers running up my spine and down my breasts till they find the right place. What if they touched me the way Father did? What would happen?

I shamelessly entice the boys at school, flirt and lead them on while hating the idea of their touch. Even Harald, my best and dearest friend, I kiss him now greedily and with anger, then push him away and call him a dirty pig. He doesn't like it and stays away from me. His mother throws me disgusted looks, but she never liked me anyway. It's all so very sad, and I don't know what it's about. Everything and everybody around me is changing.

. . .

A boy from school takes me for walks in the park. He is shy. We hold hands and kiss, but he doesn't touch my breasts and I stop going with him. I want the real adventurous ones, those that start to pull me close, rub their 'Big Bad Boy' against me and lower their hands down my belly. With those I go out again. Whoever asks first.

Slowly, we go deeper into the park to where it ends and the forest starts, big trees with low hanging branches lending ample shelter and privacy. I let them play with me as a punishment of sorts, but I don't know what or why, and the playing gets rougher. Those kisses with tongues like a cow's that stuff my whole mouth with slime till I gag are Father's tongue I feel, the way he ate and slurped, the way he drooled over me when I bent down. They disgust me, and I move my head away and encourage them to do things down my belly where I don't have to taste them. It sends shockwaves through me, and I want more, want them to slip their hand through the waistband of my skirt and down to my bare skin to touch where Father touched. When they do, it ignites my terror like a lightning strike, and a violent rage returns for they do what Father did, and they are guilty. I push them away, scream and kick, call them Father's special names, those bastards; may they burn in hell for all eternity. They are lucky I don't bite. Then I run away through the park, crying. I realize it is the fear I crave. The fear and the disgust. And some sick pleasure. But I can't be sure.

Before long nobody wants to come to the park with me or take me to the movies. Most of my time is spent window shopping or in the library where I sit, brooding and lonely.

I am a pariah, get looks of pity and ridicule, and I am

ashamed. Feverish happiness and fake laughter crumble into rage or despair at any moment. Especially when I see Harald and Isabel walk hand in hand. I pushed him away and into her arms.

Days are long and complicated. The normalness of people, kids and strollers does not fit the truth of my thoughts. Lost and out of place, I stay out late to embrace the dark. It brings out the silent world of men that sit or sleep on benches. They talk to themselves, smell of liquor or worse, huddle alone under a blanket, stare with hollow eyes and missing limbs. I feel the revulsion and the pity that others feel for me. There is an empty bench, and I sit down waiting for nothing.

Some men tell me "Go home, you're too young to be here by yourself."

Others look at me with a glint in their eyes. I can see it through the dark.

'You are just the girl for me,' they say or 'if you tell me your name, I'll show you mine.'

One man asked if I've ever been with a man before. I walked away then.

Today, a man older than Herr Rosen's age sits down next to me on a bench a bit further into the park. He is very close and tells me how beautiful I am, and he is lonely, and we should be lonely together. He puts his hand around my shoulders, asks if that's all right, and I nod my head since he is polite. Now he moves his hand further around and gently starts caressing my front. It feels almost good. He kisses me in the neck and fiddles with his right hand below his belly and I see him pull out his sausage, a 'Big Bad Boy' like the ones we sell to truckers. He takes my hand to touch it. I jolt it away. Now he slips his hand under my skirt instead and pushes me onto the bench, thrusts his body onto mine, and the full effect of his beer breath is on my face. Panic and disgust make me struggle but he lets go of me before I scream.

"Dumb cow, don't play with fire," he yells as I run away in a sweat. Close to town, I see Harald and Isabel. I stop and stay in the dark. They don't see me with all the kissing they do. They probably saw a movie and are in love. I feel betrayed, then strangely stupid. I am turning into the dumb shit Father said I was, a butcher's daughter who will become a butcher's wife.

He is still bullying me from the grave is what's happening! Bastard! I need to tell the truth, owe it to my friends and to me. I am a human garbage can, emotional carnage and full of shit is what it is. I am also still too shaky from the man's beer breath and his 'Bad Boy' to be having such serious thoughts.

Frau Graf kept leftover potatoes for me. I devour them with my fingers then run to the bathroom and vomit them back up. She doesn't say a word. Her look of disgust says it for her. I am too shaken to say anything.

It hits me like one of the thousands of mines they are warning about. All my friends are tired of me. There are none left! I am as alone as I ever was before I met the piano. Without Frau Graf that will be gone too. For a while now Frau Dietrich has not invited me to join them for the midday meal. Instead I practice the piano while they eat. Which is for the better, since I am so very angry at Isabel for stealing my Harald. Of course, I threw him at her; but that's part of my lies, isn't it?

Thoughts and logic trump emotions is what I used to think.

How wrong I was! Emotions are wildly more powerful they and merit my full attention.

Nature moves slowly. That is until an earthquake strikes, or a volcano erupts!

The neighbor's girl who has my name came home yesterday and saw a tall skinny guy run into their barn. She called police who arrived in a hurry and surrounded the property. He came out arms up, looking more like an icicle than a lamppost. That's how frozen he was and bone tired of fighting the cold of winter dressed for summer. He will languish forever in a special prison for the most dangerous guys. The police chief is under house arrest for now.

This is my chance. Don't ask me why or what, but something pulls me to that girl, Monika, for no reason other than I must follow my feet. She never went to high school, and we never met close up, and now we must. The pull is strong and must be obeyed.

She opens the door, surprised that it's me, and she just stares like I was an unknown object.

"May I come in?"

"Mama, can you come to the door? It's the neighbor's girl."

"Hello," says her Mama. It is awkward, I should just leave, but I need to be here and talk.

"I was never allowed to come near you. But I wanted to thank you for..."

"Come in. What would you need to thank us for?" Her Mama is not particularly friendly.

"When I was stolen, they called me Klara. I didn't want to be Klara, I wanted to be me. Had you not called 'Monika, time to come in,' or 'time to eat,' I would have lost the last bit of who I was. You see I, too, am called Monika."

"Why did you never come over and tell us?"

"I was not allowed and was terrified of their beatings. I imagined playing with you. But I can leave now if you want me to."

They just stand there, wordless, and I leave. Maybe they don't read the news and have no clue. For sure their manners are worse than mine.

Where will I stay now? I am seventeen years old. Somehow, I had hoped they would ask me to stay and talk, get to know each other.

Mother is out of the hospital and in prison, Father is dead. I should be delighted but feel no emotions. The relief of his death was short lived. It is late afternoon, dark shadows are claiming the last buildings in town, and I decide to visit Frau Rittenmaier and the twins for lack of something better to do. I take my bike and pedal to her house, make a detour past city hall and the little blue library. I like this town, my little town, have become a part of it, and the town is part of me. It's the people that cause me grief.

"Knock knock." The door is open, and I enter. Josef is laughing so hard he must be in pain. Martina is tickling him.

"Klara, Klara," they yell and come running my way. Maybe that's why I don't like my real name anymore. For those little kids, I am Klara, and it is meaningful. I go down on the floor and kiss them, tickle them and smother them with more kisses. Mama is coming out of her room and hugs me too.

"We missed you. Did they find the Monster?"

I nod my head and tell her about my strange visit with my namesake and her mother. How they faulted me somehow.

"Give them time. They have their own story to tell. We all do, you know. Just look around in town at all the different people."

I look at her quizzically, almost in a mocking way. What kind of a story could she have with a husband and kids? A boring one. I don't care to listen. My head is overflowing with my own. And, slightly irritated, I turn around and leave again.

17

ANGST

Days follow days, turn into weeks. At seventeen years of age, I am free to roam between the three houses of Frau Graf, Frau Dietrich and Frau Rittenmaier. Most nights I spend with Frau Graf. Time is my own, every day and every minute of my life, mine. Nobody else to think about or worry about. Each house has a place for me to sleep and food to eat. Lately, however, Frau Graf is trying to spoil it.

"If you come home late again, I will not feed you and lock the door, just so you know," she warned me the other day. "You have three families that love you, and you need to respect each one and their rules. Do you hear me?"

I grunted something in response, and she grabbed my arm.

"Did you hear me?" We stared at each other, but still I didn't respond.

"It's your Father, isn't it? He did not squeeze you. You turned into a beautiful girl, and he desired you. Please Klara, tell me the truth. I am a woman and understand all the things that can happen!"

That's what she said, and I wanted to tell her but couldn't, just couldn't. How can I tell anybody that he called me a 'good girl' and made me bend for him naked from the waist down where all the private things are?

Instead, I soak up what has been kept from me like all the things I see in store windows. I dream of making lots of money to buy those things, wear them on my head, on my feet and hang them on my ears, or eat them.

The butchery is empty, but I stay away, don't even get close. When I do, I break out in a cold sweat, almost more now than when he was alive. How can that be? They tell me I must make decisions once I am eighteen, but I keep it as far away from my thoughts as Father hanging on the hook. The memory of his swollen legs and fat little feet dangling from his corpse causes a sudden nausea. I don't even know where he is buried. I would have ground him up for the vultures, and why do I even think about him when it still agitates me so much?

What else will I do with my life? I wanted it to be a fresh start after he died, with no screams, no Rottweilers, no pain, wanted nothing left of guts and garbage; yet I create my own as if I missed it. And why do my dream shadows still run away from me? Why do they never let me catch them? I've been so lonely. Not a single boy has wanted to take me out again until today. He is new in class and hasn't heard the rumors about me. We are going out to a movie and maybe for a walk afterwards in the moonshine. He seems nice and smart, and I want so badly to behave and not freak out.

In the late afternoon, I go to Frau Rittenmaier's house and invite myself for dinner and the night. "If you could leave the back door open, please, I am going out after dinner."

"Klara, we need to have a little talk." She pouts her lips. Not a good sign. We wait till the twins are busy with a book.

"You know you are always welcome here. But you are getting older, you need to pull your weight a bit and not abuse our friendship."

What is she talking about? What the hell?

"I'll go to Frau Graf then, she'll have me." And I storm out of her house, distraught and a bit angry for not being wanted. After all we've been through together. She comes running after me, grabs me by my shoulders.

"Klara, you know we love you. What happened to you? You changed, we didn't! We want to help, that's all. Please hear me. There is nothing you could tell me that I wouldn't understand."

But I turn around and keep walking, too flustered and confused to go to anybody's house. Did I just miss a chance to tell her what happened? What if nobody will have me? Why wouldn't they? I am getting hungry, but the stores just closed. The smell from the bakery is so strong it pains me. There were times with Father and Mother when dreams of food, of made up toys and made up family had to be enough. It's not enough now. It's all about Father, isn't it? I never even think of Mother. I walk over to Harald's house, in need of a good friend, even if he kisses Isabel now, but his mother opens the door and tells me he won't be going out tonight, and for sure not with me. And she closes the door in my face!

Near the library, I sit down on a bench very close to town and to lights, utterly lost. Everything was going so well an hour ago, how can things change so fast? A very pregnant lady wobbles by on swollen ankles, trying not to topple over. How will that baby change her life? How would it change mine? Could I give it away, or would I want it? A man hobbles by on crutches. He has only one leg, the other pant leg is held up with safety pins. How come I always stared but never thought about crippled people. What do they do with their life? It must be difficult to work without the proper limbs. I look around at other people. They all have a story. I am not the only one. And, as if in a movie theatre watching the scenes go by, Monika's Mother is coming my way, Frau Schumann. I never see her, never, or maybe I never wanted to see her. She comes close, looks at me and after hesitating for just a breath or two, sits down next to me.

"I owe you an apology. It was quite a surprise to see you come to our door that time, a long time ago already, and I handled it very poorly. Sorry. Let me tell you the reason so you can understand. She takes a handkerchief out of her pocket and blows her nose, hard, folds it over twice. "You see, Hans the butcher and I were sweethearts. He got me pregnant just before he met your Mother." She uses the handkerchief to wipe her tears.

"She isn't my Mother."

"I know that now. Have been reading up on it. But all this time I thought my Hans was still living next door, without ever talking to me or his own child. I never even saw him. He knew I was pregnant and seemed ecstatic. And then that woman came into his life and she was pregnant at about the same time I was. Ach. Those were hard times on top of hard times. And that is my story and my daughter's story."

She gets up and leaves me with tears in my eyes. There are so many stories inside all of us. I never thought she had any, being just the neighbor. The new boy Peter is probably waiting for me at the movie theater, but I can't get up. I tremble to the fibers of my flesh and don't know if it's from the cold or from her story, and my tummy is begging me for food. When an elderly man with a cane places his skinny ass next to mine, lights a cigarette and blows the smoke in my face, I get up and march on to Frau Graf for a meal and my bed. I am barely in time. She is dangling the key in her hand to show me how lucky I am. We eat together in silence. Herr Rosen is not here, and I miss his presence, his comforting voice, his polished shoes. There are lots of dishes in the sink today, leftover from lunch and even from the morning, but my book is too exciting to offer my help. It's called 'Rebecca' by Daphne du Maurier, and I am just getting into it. It's good to share someone else's misery; it lightens my own.

"Good night," she says later, "thank you for your amazing help and friendship." Is she being sarcastic? What's going on with everybody. They used to feel sorry for me and offered their help and love.

"You are welcome," I shout behind her as she slams the door. Slams it! Maybe she and Frau Rittenmaier are both having their period. Mine gets me very annoyed. I feel dumb for not knowing why and dumber for not asking. And I remember that I never asked her to tell me the rest of her story with Herr Rosen. She might think I don't care. Maybe I don't.

18

MY OWN BEST FOOL

It was a noisy night. Heavy winds rattled the wooden shutters outside the windows and whipped and bent the trees. Their tired branches scraped the walls of the house till it creaked and moaned. I woke up from the noise and to the smell of no coffee. I hope she is not sick. I need my coffee. I put on long stockings, hook them into my garter belt and throw on the rest of my clothes. Frau Graf is coming out of her bedroom.

"Are you feeling all right?" I ask very caringly.

"Never better, especially once you make the coffee. I'll sleep in more often from now on." And she yawns and stretches, arms high up with folded hands, then goes to the window to look out. She is certainly not moving towards the kitchen. I guess I'll need to take care of the coffee myself.

She stopped driving me to school after they found the Monster, and I take my bike like other kids, rain or snow. Will I need to make my own coffee from now on? I so love to be taken care of. But I do brew a full pot and drink a cup.

"Good-bye, have a good day," I say and leave. Outside, I

turn around to wave. She stares down at me with sadness in her eyes and does not wave back.

Every day is a glorious day at school. I ignore all boys and grin all day long. Doctor Stahl, skinny little guy, is annoyed that I still haven't turned in a report that he considers of great importance.

"What's going on? It's your future, not mine," he has told me more than once.

I keep quiet. Yes, it's all mine so shut up. Silently, I call him a truly mean word even though he is very nice, really. At times, it's as if I were two different people that don't like each other, sullen the one, euphoric the other, and I can't find my own place in between.

At Isabel's house, they eat while I play the piano. Yes, at least they still let me practice. But there is a stress in the air, looks that come my way, whispers. Am I imagining things? I leave, haven't gone to my afternoon classes for a while, walk aimlessly around town instead, buy a pretzel, but can't get into it. What a waste of time. My park bench is empty, and I claim it as my own. It's the prime bench for people watching without being seen. It seems that other people's stories are getting more important while mine is starting to bore me. Even the one about my shadow family. They were nice people. Haven't thought about them for a long time; barely any shadows are left, only a small pain in my heart because they never tried to find me. I know that's wrong, but I like to pity me. It gives me a perverse pleasure, one of the few I have left. And why am I always my own best fool?

. . .

My behind is turning into an ice float. I sit on it, drifting slowly into the ocean like an old Eskimo woman. There is no pain. What a nice way to die! Would anybody miss me?

Frau Dietrich, Nicholas and Isabel walk out of the library. Nicholas comes out first, a couple of books in one hand, the other pulling Frau Dietrich whose other arm is entwined with Isabel. A lovely picture. I feel left out. What do I truly know about them? Nothing. I wanted to belong, be Isabel's friend but never was. Nicholas mostly ignores me now, Herr and Frau Dietrich are polite, but only just. Even gentle Frau Rittenmaier told me off!

And the guys with their whispers behind my back, they did what I wanted them to do, no more. Their tongues and their touches, it all was because of Father. His touch terrorized me, and I lost my mind. But he is dead, and whatever is happening now is my own fault!

I am getting terribly sad and start crying heavy tears of a loneliness so deep and desperate I run far into the park to hide my shaking body in the damp and moldy darkness of a tree, the only living thing left for me to lean on.

When I am emptied of tears and cold to the core, I walk back into town. It is dark now, stores are closed, people are at home, curtains closed. I have no home and no family. The little I had, I messed it up. It is even too late to go to Frau Graf. Her door will be locked.

19

BLOOD CURDLING SCREAMS

Without knowing where to go, I simply follow my feet. And my feet bring me to the house of horrors. It looks down at me in the dark of the night, a silent, gigantic corpse hanging on a hook. I want to run, but my feet do not move. Ice cold fingers grab me by the neck. They are Father's, I can smell him, and I vomit as he slowly twists my head. It cracks like ice, and I try to scream but can't, instead a blood curdling howl echoes through the night, and the neighbors hear my howl, from a wild animal they think, but they see me and help me into their house.

Neither one asks any questions. They lead me to an old flowered sofa in blue, help me sit down and put up my legs. Frau Schumann takes off my shoes. I am shaking violently and nearly kick her. Monika covers me with a blanket. I can't stop the shaking, and she brings me her winter coat to put on top. Her Mama offers me a cup of tea that is still hot and turns on the kettle to boil more water. But I fall asleep, dreamless, and don't wake up till early in the morning.

Monika is dressed, buttering a slice of bread. She folds it over to eat on the way.

"I have to run. Hope you feel better."

"Would you like me to call you Monika or Klara?" asks Frau Schumann, snuggled tightly into an old pink robe which has seen better times.

"Klara, please."

She goes outside to the outhouse, and I hope not for long. My bladder is bursting. I see a cluttered living room filled with photos and paintings on every wall and doilies on every surface with keepsakes. A blue and yellow throw blanket on the sofa looks hand knitted by one of the two. She is back now, and I go next.

I return to the aroma of freshly brewed coffee. It wafts into my nostrils like a life- giving elixir. My only meal yesterday was a pretzel.

"There is also leftover cereal; I can heat it up if you want to."

"Just some coffee, please." I stand uncomfortably in the middle of the room.

"Did you have dinner last night?"

"I don't think so. No, I didn't."

"Then I will heat you some cereal, and you will eat it for me." She offers me a chair and I sit down watching her heat it up. She is a pretty woman with blond curls that end in a touch of gold from the morning sun and a well-shaped behind for sitting. Like most older women, I guess, except for Mother who is a bag of bones. She brings me a bowl of cereal, sits down across from me and watches me eat. And I eat and watch her. She is full of sadness. It shows not just by the eyes but in her movements. Sadness makes us lethargic, drags us down like wearing a girdle that's too tight. Makes me wonder, do I look sad to others?

"Tell me what's going on in your head since your Father died. It might be easier to talk to me than to your friends, you know."

"I am fine. Something scared me last night."

"You howled as if the Rottweiler was chasing you."

"Whatever happened to the one that disappeared?" I ask her, suddenly curious.

"He was put down, I guess, years ago. They were made vicious by being chained all their lives, poor things."

"Yes, and poor me! Walking past them to the outhouse was spine chilling each and every day of my life."

She is quiet, does not want to push me. I like that.

"May I look at your photos?"

"Please do while I get dressed."

I finish the last bite and get up, take my plate to the kitchen. It opens into a small vegetable and herb garden. I can't see my house from this side and am glad.

Most of the photos show group pictures of a large family. Adults and children stare out into the living room like statues, impenetrable and joyless. These are very old photos, black and brownish from age, when people wore dark clothes with lace around neck and sleeves. She must have inherited their doilies. They are in the photos and now on her tables. The photos with Monika and her Mama are more recent, and they have a third person in it, a man with his arms slung around the two of them in a tight hug. A tall, handsome man with an easy smile, his chin leaning on Mama's head, while she is leaning into him contented as a baby. Monika has her arms around him with a look like 'he is all mine.'

"The man, is it Hans? You look so happy," I ask when she comes back out, nicely dressed in dark stockings, a pleated skirt and a heavy sweater. She pours herself another cup of coffee but doesn't sit down.

"No. Remember, he never saw me after that woman appeared, your Mother. I was pregnant then with his child."

"Who is it then?"

"I got married when Monika was four years old. Ach! Such a good man and a loving stepfather. Monika adored him. He is dead."

He is dead, I think. And then I know. Father killed him too.

She puts down her cup and fetches her coat.

"I need to go to work and you need to come along, somebody in town is worried about you." She sees me hesitate and ready to argue.

"No discussion. Come along now, big girl."

On the way to town I tell her why I can't go back to my friends. How everybody suddenly lets me down. She lectures me on how to be considerate, and if people take care of me, I need to take care of them, too.

"Think of it that way," she points out, "if you took care of somebody your age, day after day, love them and feed them, what would you like to get from them? And it's not money. You are a lucky girl. My Monika, she goes to work already. She would have loved to go to high school, but we needed the money. We still do."

When we part ways, I have the strangest feeling that she is kind of my stepmother, and Monika is my half- sister. After all, the butcher, one of them for sure, was her real father, and that makes us family if we choose to be.

It is early in the morning when I head to Frau Graf, worried, unsettled and ashamed. I ring the doorbell and hear her run to the door and open it. With red teary eyes she hugs me into her warm nightgown, its yeasty night smells lingering in the blue cotton fabric.

"Girl, you are alive, we all worried so much." She plants a juicy kiss on my cheek, then holds me away by my arms and yells "foolish girl, what you did was wrong and mean. Get ready for school now, no time to eat, and after school you get your butt right here on this sofa, do you hear me?"

"Yes, I do, you are yelling right in my ear."

That's how it feels to be a dog whimpering with its tail between its legs for chewing up the slippers.

The day is extremely long. Why should I sit on her sofa? What if I want to stand? Teachers talk, and I don't hear a word. Herr Stahl, our physics teacher, wears his grey tie with black stripes. His other one is black with grey stripes. Why can't he be more adventurous? Add color? Doesn't he know we stare at him for a whole hour twice a week? He threatens something about my homework, but I can't process it. Will she still welcome me in her house? I am a nervous wreck, deeply worried. The minute school is over I bike to her house to get it over with. Then I stop and very slowly take the stairs that lead to her apartment, counting each step seven times for luck.

· · ·

The doorbell is too loud and shrill. A most irritating sound. Frau Graf opens the door.

"Come in, get yourself some food and sit down."

She made my favorite soup, lentils with pieces of beef in it. I eat a lot and thank her but am not ready to say 'sorry, it's all my fault.' Then I sit down on her old sofa squirming like a worm, worried she might banish me from her house forever, and I whimper "why are you so mean?"

She keeps pacing around. Her presence is too big for the room, and I wish she'd sit down.

"Girl," she finally says, stopping in front of me and looming over me like a general. "Girl, we pulled you out of the gutter, and you jumped right back in. Want to be a gutter snake? Her finger is pointing at me, her arm cutting through the air like a butcher's razor-sharp knife. "Rumor has it that your schoolwork is suffering, young men are drooling over you, and you like their drool. Do you realize as a pregnant girl you cannot finish high school? You might yet end up as a butcher's wife just as your Father wished! If you prove him right, he'll smile in his grave."

"How can I get pregnant when I don't know how it works?" Here, I said it! It wasn't hard.

"Oh my. That's a different conversation. Let's do that first. As a matter of fact, I won't let you leave this house or look at any boys without understanding human plumbing."

She stares at me for a while thinking 'she doesn't know? She really doesn't?' Then she sits down and minces no words telling me about boys and their ways and about us girls. In and out like a plug in the wall. Should have thought of it myself.

That's what Father tried to do and the others in the park. She enjoys the topic and continues.

"I call it a pussy. It's one of many endearing words regarding the girly parts of a woman. The proper terms are penis and vagina when you talk to others. And if Father did what I believe he had in mind but didn't quite finish, - or did he? - that's bad, but with the right person it is very good, remember that. Don't let Father harm you from beyond the grave."

"He got me wet. He might have peed on me."

"No. He ejaculated. That stuff is what gets us pregnant if it gets inside."

"It's a bunch of disgusting goo."

"We girls have our own gooey stuff."

".....you are saying life is made of sticky gooey stuff? We make googoo eyes at each other, then comes the boy goo, the girl goo, and then the babies? When I look at you, Frau Graf, I think you are made of a much tougher yet very intricate stuff, being so amazing. I am glad you are the one to introduce me to it. Frau Rittenmaier and Frau Dietrich would not have been so clear. They are more ladylike and delicate of nature. In fact, I doubt I would have learned anything at all."

"More ladylike! You can't beat around the bush with such a topic, girl; you either get it right or you don't. And if procreation were more complicated, humans would be extinct. That's how stupid we are. Think of yourself, how you've been acting lately. Foolish and mean. You should be ashamed. My girl, you'll spend all next week with me! Your last chance to get it right. After school, you will spill your thoughts and tears into a journal. Don't think too hard, let them bubble out and set them free. Think of your shadow family, invite them back in and listen, listen to them carefully; they are not gone. They might dream about you every day of their lives. You need them, and they need you more. Do you hear me? Those deep wounds of yours need cleaning out more than your ears. Don't let them fester in your fake new happiness. Girl, you can't bake a cake from a pile of shit."

20

A CHEESECAKE AND A HEAP OF SHIT

There are new rules now. A movie once a month. A friend once a week to play board games with. I'll have to learn those. And whoever takes me to a movie must pick me up at the house for inspection. No twilight encounters of any kind! (I turn bright red. Does everybody in town know what I did in the park?) But it feels strangely like a lifeline has been thrown my way, the rules being the safety net that will protect me mostly from myself.

Frau Graf is never out of words, and I quickly interrupt before she takes another breath and thinks of another rule.

"I don't know a word you just said. I am too full of nothing really, just all the garbage in my head. I am emotionally crippled."

"The hell you are. You need a good night's sleep. Now how about you and I bake a cake, or maybe let's just buy one. I want to celebrate this day. We know you are, or could be, quite magnificent. You need to try and believe it too.

And together, like mother and daughter, we shop. We have never done that before. She holds me by my hand and half drags me along so that I won't look in every window. It feels awfully good. We get a large cheesecake at the bakery and pick up some Swiss chocolate to nibble on the way.

Herr Rosen is at home when we return, and the potatoes are already boiling. He still wears his fancy suit with a handkerchief folded in its breast pocket and shiny shoes. Even the shoelaces are clean unlike most people's laces which are knotted together from old ones. They kiss, we shake hands, I set the table, then help clean carrots. Beef cubes are simmering in a pot with onions, and the smell fills my eyes with tears and my nose starts dripping, and I wipe it with my sleeve.

"Disgusting," she yells. "Go do your homework. It's past due. You want to go to college, don't you?"

I nod my head and go in my room. The homework is easy. Why did it take such a painful kick in the butt to get it done? The sweet smells of food and the rattling of silverware lure me back into the kitchen. I am starved from barely any food in the last 24 hours, and the cheesecake is staring at me. I stare back. My picking finger twitches like Herr Rosen's nose.

"Don't you dare!" Frau Graf threatens, her finger in my face.

Herr Rosen is licking his fingers after testing the meat and watching us, his eyebrows raised just so.

"Did you ever get to do naughty things like normal kids?" I shake my head, sadly, "of course not."

"Then go for it. Be a pig." Frau Graf looks at him amused and adds,

"Well then but scrub your hands first."

She grabs him by the sleeve and pulls him out of the

kitchen. "Let her be," she says, and to me, "we won't look. But you better leave some for us."

The cheesecake ends up all over my face and hands. He grins seeing how much I ate, while she comes towards me, her tongue far out and panting like a dog, threatening to lick the crumbs off my face. I quickly wash up in the sink, and we get dinner to the table.

"I am too full to eat, but don't worry, I left room for more cheesecake."

"With a spoon, this time," they respond in unison.

After dinner we sit down. Frau Graf and Herr Rosen on the old sofa, while I plant myself on a chair. He unfolds the newspaper, then quickly folds it back together and puts it down. "Tell us what happened last night!"

And Frau Graf hits her fingers on the coffee table as if it were a piano and says: "when you stayed out and worried us to death."

"Last night? That seems so long ago. I guess after school I didn't know where to go, what to do. I felt not welcomed and sat on a park bench for hours, got hungry and cold and started walking aimlessly through the night. Ended up at the butchery without realizing it. And there I stood, seized by such terror it paralyzed me, couldn't move or scream. I swear I smelled him and felt his hand on my neck. The neighbors heard what they thought was a wounded animal. They checked and saw me stand and howl and took me in, Monika and her Mother, and moments later I was sound asleep on their sofa."

"Your Father, that miserable son of a bitch, ach, what a heap of shit he was, he'll continue to scare you until he is properly buried, not shoved under the rug. It's time to deal with it. I will help you," threatens Frau Graf.

"He killed Monika's stepfather." It popped out of my mouth without thinking and they look at me like 'what is she talking about?'

"Their walls in the living room are plastered with photos. Frau Schumann was married you know, and they clearly seemed to be very happy, the three of them. He died suddenly. She didn't tell me how, but I know that Father was involved. One of our Rottweilers disappeared around the time she told me he died."

"You could be a detective," says Herr Rosen. "Not saying you'd be a good one, but who knows? You have the nose of a bloodhound."

"Do not!"

"I mean your instinct, silly girl, not your little nose. And just out of curiosity, I'll check out what her stepfather died of. It's easy enough to look at old police records."

"I'd like that, please. Now I am exhausted. If you don't mind, I'll go to sleep."

"I do mind. Look at all the dirty dishes! It's nasty to leave for the morning. Daniel, will you help clean the table, please?"

He does before returning to his newspaper, while Frau Graf washes, and I dry.

"Tomorrow, you'll wash, and I dry. Sweet dreams."

"Sweet dreams," echoes Herr Rosen, and I say the same and retire.

· · ·

It is a night of tossing and turning. My brain is working at high speed without spinning a single coherent thought. There are visions of a flat empty landscape of pure white snow, reaching far into the horizon with sudden bursts of brilliant colors that vanish before my eyes. I cannot catch them and cannot breathe. Slowly, I wake up. At least there were no sausages.

I am the first one up and put the kettle on, grind the coffee and inhale this sweet smell of life's happy juice that always seems to smell better than it tastes. Then I pour me a cup. It is Sunday, the only day of the week to not go to school, and maybe I can do some thinking.

What in the world? What the devil? Frau Graf is dressed in old tired looking black pants, which are tied around the bottom. Nobody wears long pants except to ski or hike, or maybe to hide one's unshapely legs. Right behind her comes Herr Rosen in the same old pants and a pullover the color of vomit, frayed along the neck.

"Good morning. What a pleasure to wake up to coffee smells."

They fill their cups, then we eat our simple breakfast of days old buns with butter and jam. I stare at them.

"Is everything alright?" I ask.

They grin at me. Something is up their sleeves.

21

MUSIC OF THE UNIVERSE

Herr Rosen takes a big bite out of his bun, chews leisurely and then he says:

"Let me tell you our plan for the day."

We never had a plan for the day. Are they going to teach me another lesson? How many more lessons do I need?

"You need fresh air. We will take you to our special place where Frau Graf and I first met. It is a bit of a drive and a long hike. I hope you have good shoes and even better stamina."

He talks the way I imagine him talking to criminals, and I answer meekly "Yes, Herr Rosen." His unshaven chin and crummy clothes make him look strangely attractive.

We make buttered bread to take along for the midday meal. Frau Graf adds cinnamon stars and the rest of the chocolate she bought yesterday. We dress warmly and leave into the sunny day under a clear blue sky and roads that are finally free of snow. It's a long drive. We pass it in silence except for Herr Rosen's hiccups for the first half hour and the VWs anguished shrieks when climbing uphill.

Herr Rosen stops in a small town similar in size to ours, with the bakery, dairy, butcher, shoemaker and greengrocer built around the marketplace, the apothecary and post office a bit to the side. Homes form a belt around the stores. Rolling farmland reaches beyond and up on hills and into valleys as far as I can see, which is not far because the hills are in the way and the morning fog has settled in the valleys. We park the car next to a small path, Herr Rosen takes the backpack with our lunch, and the three of us start on our hike up my first mountain. We fit side by side and Frau Graf holds my hand. After about an hour's hike, the path curves into a steep incline, and she lets go of it. No doubt she noticed my efforts to be pulled. She is a clever woman and lucky. He is pushing her now with both his hands on her hefty butt which, it seems, he enjoys as much as she does. I notice her extra wiggles for his benefit and feel strangely happy.

After about two or more hours of going straight up without meeting another soul, we get to a lookout. It's a small place with boulders and rocks, and right around those rocks is a cliff big enough for one person. I take my turn and here it is, their lake, deep down, dark and mysterious. That's where they fell in love and she into the water, and he after her to save her life.

"We should put a marker on this spot in honor of your love," I say.

"No no no. It would destroy its solitude and beauty. Look around, we are alone in the world. This place invites thoughtfulness and dreams of peace. Can you feel it?" She asks.

"I have dreams of peeing in peace, please, I really feel it."

"Go ahead." They nod their heads, and I take off, straight up. It is quickly getting steeper, and the path gets lost. I start to climb over large rocks. The next cliff is precariously hanging over me, and I walk away from it around what now looks like a high mountain. The fog has lifted. There is no view of the lake, but the snow level is right ahead of me. Must be the northern side. I pee, get a tiny sprinkle on my shoes, wish I had better equipment like men but get disgusted at the thought. I have got to stop imagining sausages; would so like to eat them again one day.

There is no sound. A gentle wind is playing with branches, a tiny noise maybe from a mouse or rabbit running over a twig. It is a silence the way I've never heard it. Or never Not heard it, since it is silent. Deep down in the valley, tiny dollhouses dot the land with tiny faceless people. Their movements are barely visible, but each one is on a mission. Each one thinks they are important. I am one of those people, one of too many to count, like an ant. Towns are big ant hills, that's all. I am an ant and give myself too much importance and not enough to others.

Slowly, the sounds of the universe become audible. I can feel it almost more than hear it, filling the space with the sound of the air, the dust, our pulsating hearts, a kind of vibration and whirring like a faraway choir from the Milky Way with billions of ants pounding the forest floor with their feet. Silence is not empty. It is filled with its own silent sounds, powerful if you truly listen. It becomes almost painful to bear, these many tiny chaotic sounds hitting against my ears. I go back down, slowly, didn't realize how steep it was to get here.

· · ·

They stand close to each other, whispering. They were certainly not bored without me.

"That was a long pee, like over an hour," she says.

"I tried it standing up." They stare at my clothes and shoes to check for wetness, until I laugh.

"It was amazing up there, so quiet I could hear the things that have no sound. Did you bring me here to realize how unimportant I am compared to the world?"

"No," she says. "We came for our anniversary and didn't want to leave you home alone. But if your insignificance seems significant up here it means that usually you give too much thought to yourself and not enough to others."

"Frau Graf, my love, you are not only beautiful but so clever. Now shut up and let's eat." Herr Rosen slaps a big kiss somewhere on her face. And all three of us sit down on rocks that best fit our bottoms and eat. I especially appreciate the cinnamon stars and the chocolate, having years of catching up to do.

We don't talk about anything, like the rest of their love story which I am suddenly very curious to hear. It's disappointing. They just sit on their rocks and look happy.

When the last of the food is gone, Frau Graf suggests that I might want to scream my sorrows over the cliff and into the world the way she did so long ago.

"Ignore us, go, let go of it. We won't listen."

I get up, barely peek down the cliff when a powerful vertigo pulls me towards the water. It's the weight of Father's naked corpse trying to push me down, one of his fat legs dangling next to me. I take a quick step back and nearly faint. Herr Rosen grabs ahold of me, and I sit down for a short rest. Then we hike back to town and drive home in silence, thinking our thoughts and watching the day move into the horizon. After eating our usual meal of a salad, dark bread and whatever goes with it, pickles on the side, Herr Rosen opens a bottle of wine. They drink to each other on their special day and leave the dishes to me. I clean up and retire early to read my book 'Rebecca.' When I wake up in the morning, my body aches from the long hike in places I never knew existed.

Doctor Stahl's freshly shaved jowls quiver from happiness, and his eyes glaze over when I hand in my long overdue homework. I owe him big time for his patience and his belief in me and hang on his every word, my brain being in high gear from all the fresh air. He is truly one of the few men that have helped me throughout these years. After school, I look for Isabel without knowing what to say and why. She is already on her bike, and I wave to her. She stops and waits.

"Isabel," I say gazing into her beautiful big blue eyes that I had all but forgotten, and on a quick impulse I put an arm around her. "Isabel," I say again, "you are ..... I am sorry but I have to run." And I run to get my bike and pedal away, never looking back. It's the first hug I ever gave instead of got, and it feels like an immensely big deal.

"Frau Graf, hello." I hug her also. My second hug today. "It takes courage to hug you, I hope you appreciate it."

"Courage? Why for heaven's sake? Look at me, soft, a body like a mattress to sink into, with breasts others can only dream of. I am a goddess."

"I will pray for you. It's not your body I am talking about, it is your persona. You are a bit scary as you well know."

"Yes, my dear, we both are. We are very much alike. Two

goddesses."

"Delusional," I mumble, looking down at my body that's more scarecrow than goddess. Holy Moses. I look again. It seems my breasts are finally starting to blossom. She is watching me and laughs.

"You've been attracting boys like flies. I hear about things. We better buy you a bra. It makes your breasts a bit harder to get to." My face breaks into a bright red blush.

We eat a light midday meal of buttered potatoes, fried egg and spinach. Then I do the dishes while she is getting ready for her first student.

"Do your journal," she reminds me. "And your homework, but the journal first."

I disappear into my little room with my bed and a desk. It is their study and doesn't have any frills. 'Words,' she said, 'whatever pops up.'

Music,' comes to mind and the next words start flowing like musical notes. Man goo, boy goo, flies, Frau Rittenmaier, Rottweiler, the universe, ants, war, piano, terror, Father, lipstick, infinite, nothing, cabbage, vagina, meat, blood, snow, sister.' I stop with 'sister.' It has such a beautiful ring to it, and because the next word would be sausage. I do not want 'sausage' in my journal.' Then I finish reading 'Rebecca.'

Herr Rosen gets home in time for dinner. He is spending the night, and I like it. His presence makes the world seem safe, even more so than Frau Graf who could be a police chief and a prison guard all at once. The table is nicely set. The plates don't match, but each one is gold rimmed with its own intricate pattern and striking colors. Frau Graf loves things that match in their beauty rather than dull stuff that matches only in their dullness. Cold cuts, cheeses and olives are ready, and the breadbasket is filled with the dark, nutty kind of bread. Tonight, there is also a cucumber salad with dill.

"How are you two ladies?"

"I had a terrible student today but got a hug from our girl here. It made up for it."

"And I handed in my homework and hugged Isabel."

"You hug everybody now but me!" complains Herr Rosen. "What's the matter with you?" I quickly run and hug him too, one armed and half assed, and quickly run away again, blushing.

"The hike yesterday, can we do that again? The mountain made me think. If you want me to think more and harder, you could take me on more hikes until you think I've done enough thinking and consider me to be quite perfect. Then could we maybe have another cheesecake?"

"What do you think, Wolf. Shall we do that?"

"Absonoodley. We could even get a cheesecake between thoughts."

We eat, we chat, we clean up. Sounds boring? Only if you never ate, chatted and cleaned up with people you love. It's a time filled with humor, a lot of it my own! We laugh so hard she calls my funny! That's a first! He calls me 'meshugge,' Hebrew for 'a bit crazy'. Tomorrow's muscle ache in my face will be such pleasant pain.

When we retire to the living room Herr Rosen stops laughing. He pulls out his handkerchief, coughs up a good amount of stuff and twitches his nose, ready to tell us today's news.

. . .

"Herr Dietrich and I looked at the death of Herr Schumann, Monika's stepfather. He simply disappeared into the backyard, and the chief of police cleared it as a death by natural causes. Yes, the same chief of police. It is very troubling and suspicious. We need to interrogate him again. Please, until you hear from me or Herr Dietrich, do not talk about it. Frau Schumann might get distraught over maybe nothing. I am only telling you because of your very good instincts, and you can keep secrets more than anyone I know."

"Admit it, I might be a great detective."

"We'll see."

"Maybe one day I could interview Mother. Haven't seen her since she is in jail."

"You have never visited her?"

"Of course not. She is only nice compared to Father! If you compare shit to shit, it's still shit." I get a quiet but glaring rebuke from Frau Graf.

"Well said," says Herr Rosen. To which he gets the same glaring look.

Tonight, the white snow of my dreams shows patches of grey and black filth, garbage pokes out and bright red drops of blood drip to the ground as I slowly awaken to these new haunting images. What does it mean?

In the morning, I ask Frau Graf if I might go home with Isabel today because I hugged her without a reason.

"I won't stay long and won't play the piano and will do the journal right afterwards. Please? Just to clear the air."

"Well then, from one goddess to another, go clear the air."

She shakes her head like 'why do you need a reason to hug, why do you need to clear the air over giving a hug. Girl, why do you think so hard?'

22

THE CRIES OF THE DEAD

"Isabel, wait for me," I call to her after school. "Isabel, please, I am so sorry."

"Come home with me," is all she says, calm and with kindness. And I follow her on my bike.

"Hello Mama, look who is here."

"Klara. It's been a while."

"I can't stay long. Frau Graf wants me to go straight to her after school."

"I know. We have all been in touch with each other."

They talk behind my back? Gossip and scheme?

"Don't be upset. We worry because we care, that's all." And she welcomes me with a hug, kisses my head, tells us the midday meal is almost ready and asks Isabel to finish mashing the potatoes.

"Add a bit more butter," she says, "and set the table for five. Frau Graf won't mind if you're late." Then she moves to the living room with me in tow, sits down on the elegant teak colored sofa and pats the seat next to her. It's very formal and I'd worry if it weren't for her kind eyes.

"Let's talk before we eat. How is that?" I nod my head and sit where she patted.

"Do you remember the first time you came to our home? Isabel was in heaven. 'That girl that was stolen. That girl whose mother put burn marks on her back and her father was worse. That girl that knew next to nothing of the outside world.' You intrigued her, and she dreamt to be your friend. Nicholas thought he'd have another big sister, maybe a nicer one than Isabel." I smile at that.

"You grew up so dreadfully alone it must be hard to make friends; we get it. And now you see Isabel and Harald be in love. Talk to them. Talking and listening is what friends do and family. About anything, even silly little things. With Nicholas? Throw a few balls with him or play chess, let him teach you, he'd love that. And observe how we live, how we help each other around the house. We feel left out of your life as totally as we invited you into ours. We don't want you to be just a guest, Klara."

I am deeply wounded but hear the love oozing out of every word. They want me to belong while I cut them out. How can that be? What can I do? I press my arms around her, dig my head into her shoulder and let my tears swim in my eyes. Tears of relief – they still love me - but mostly from onions. It's going to be liver served with oodles of onions! Yeah!

Nicholas comes storming in and is the first to sit down. "Yummy, liver, red cabbage and mashed potatoes." I ask her how she cooks the cabbage.

"With onions, caraway seeds and red wine vinegar. During apple season, I cut in an apple."

The mail is flying through the mail slot and she picks it up and puts it on Herr Dietrich's place. She likes to keep things neat and ready for him including herself. When she hears him approach the front door, she peeks into the mirror and pats her hair and chews her lip. Doesn't really change anything. I guess it's the thought that counts.

A moment later he joins us. He bought his first new car and comes home for the midday meal more often now. He had his hair cut, his curls are gone, and he looks serious, like a real police officer. I miss his curls. They added spice to him in a kind of attractive, cheerful way.

"Hello, stranger, where have you been? You look different." He kisses his wife before loosening his tie and sitting down.

"You too. Without the curls, you are intimidating. Makes it hard to apologize for all the years you helped me. I don't believe I ever thanked any of you."

"I noticed," yells Nicholas, and I give him a sad smile.

"What would have happened to me without all of you? The piano was my first friend. It saved my life thanks to Frau Rittenmaier. Later you and Frau Graf were so kind, and I used you like a lifeboat."

"How do you do that?" squeaks Nicholas.

"You grab hard and hold on for dear life. The boat itself does not matter. You did not matter. I did not know that's what I did all these many years. It's as if a new window just opened into the world and I see you for the first time."

"So, what happened to you? What changed?" Asks Herr Dietrich. They stop eating to search my face, Nicholas, his mouth full of mashed potatoes, stops chewing.

"Frau Graf, Herr Rosen and I went for a long hike up a mountain yesterday. I looked far down, felt like a wee wriggly worm, a mere speck of dust. It made me think about life and my place in it. I am not very important. There was a silence so deep yet filled with sounds, and now I must sound like a fool."

"Not too much, but a bit," laughs Herr Dietrich. They are all eating and chewing again.

Frau Dietrich admits she hears such music also when she is alone in nature. She calls it the music of the universe.

"That's what I called it. I felt so insignificant, it humbled me. I am one of millions, like ants really, and we all count. Well, some more than others I'm sure."

"That's for sure," agrees Herr Dietrich. "That's for sure."

Dinner is over. He gets up, puts on his hat, pulls up his wife's chin for a kiss and leaves again. I am ready for the piano but instead stack the dishes and carry them to the kitchen, start washing them. Nobody says a word because it is the way it should have been all these years. Isabel takes a towel to help dry, and I smile at her. 'How is Harald?' I want to ask but don't. It's my pride, not the pain, which suddenly seems to be gone.

"Why do people turn out the way they do?" I ask Frau Graf when I get home. "How much do bad parents or good parents matter? Good parents teach us things all day long and thinking for ourselves requires less thought. One might even get tired of listening and tired of thinking. But that would make good parents bad parents. Bad parents, however......"

Frau Graf seems relieved when the bell rings and her next student arrives. I may have overwhelmed her with so many questions that require deep thoughts. She starts her lesson, and I disappear into the safety of her study. And yes, that's it.

Good parents make kids feel safe. Safe and wanted. And they laugh. Laughing might be the most important ingredient. After cheesecake.

· · ·

Herr Rosen comes home early for dinner and the night. Something happened. He already changed into his pajamas and wears Frau Graf's robe and paces the room mumbling and grunting with his deep voice, his arms moving as if he were arguing or from Italy.

"Spit it out, Daniel, what is it?" Asks Frau Graf.

"Ach, God almighty, we just questioned the police chief, and he pretends he has no clue as to Herr Schumann's disappearance. 'It was too long ago' he claims. But he is lying, the bastard. You should have seen him sweat and wriggle under our questions. He was scared. We took him into custody. He is too much of a flight risk now. Damnit. We might have to dig up the yard."

"Maybe he had bad parents," I suggest.

"What are you babbling about?"

"I have a theory that people have problems because of their parents."

"Bullshit. Mine weren't all that great either, trust me."

"And see what happened! You are my living proof." I shake my finger at him.

"Well," he grunts, "maybe your parents were bad because of you. Bad kids drive parents crazy." He points his finger at me, and we grin.

"Sorry I didn't help you," I yell into the kitchen.

"Thank you for keeping me entertained," she yells back.

There is so much more to life than meets the eye. My fake parents were horrid, and I don't steal or murder. Well, I almost murdered Father, but don't hold it against me.

· · ·

While chewing on a leftover pork bone in the kitchen, the delicious juices drooling down my chin, I offer to visit Mother and find out about the Rottweiler and Herr Schumann.

"Let's go together, you and I," he says. "How about tomorrow?" That's fine with me.

I wash my hands, get comfortable on the worn old sofa and start reading 'Oliver Twist.' I like books about abuse, compare theirs with mine, and feel good that there are so many of us. There is a certain strength in numbers.

The night is turbulent. A strong wind hisses and hollers around the corners, slamming shutters that weren't properly fastened, and my dreams are as turbulent as the weather but more frightening. It's the same landscape as before but the snow is gone, and arms and legs are sticking out of the dirt crying for help. I wake up in a cold sweat and to my own muffled screams trying to run away but my legs won't move.

"You woke us up as much as the wind," Frau Graf complains in the morning. Herr Rosen wants to know what all those screams and the moaning were about.

"Do you remember any of it? Your dreams are really quite amazing."

"Yes. They are in there! In our backyard. Arms and legs were sticking out of the ground." And then I remember what Mother told me.

"Mother said they were buried in the back yard where the soil is soft, and the cries of the dead can't be heard. But she did not mention a third body."

23

CACKLING AND SMOLDERING

"Let's go see her right now." We grab our coats, take an umbrella and leave.

It's not a long drive to the prison, not in a brand-new blue VW that still smells of clean. His old one croaked one last time then kicked the bucket.

With a smile Herr Rosen shows his credentials to the guard and we go in. He always smiles at everybody, and the guard smiles back, like a quick puff of pleasantry; an easy thing to do. I will try to smile more and add my own puffs.

Mother shares her cell with one other woman.

"She has a motor mouth, this one, goes a mile a minute and can't shut the hell up, bitch. She laughs and slaps my back with dumb jokes, it drives me up the wall," she tells us the moment she arrives in the visitor's room. "I want to stuff her mouth with her stinky underwear or strangle her with her stockings, but she is way stronger. Maybe during the night someday."

Mother looks well, content even and younger, as if the extra pounds filled in most of her wrinkles. That roommate is good for her, and I hope she will get used to jokes and friendliness. Already she talks like a motor mouth herself.

"Do you like it here? I mean, do you like it better than at the butcher's store?"

"It's a relief to be here. I am free. We have a library, and I love to read. All the time in the world is mine now. The toilet stinks less than the outhouse. I could never go back."

"I can't either. The house is like a coffin and gives me chills when I get too close. Do you know whatever happened to the other Rottweiler, the one that died many years ago?

"Fritz said he had to shoot him. He attacked a man."

"But he was always chained."

"What is it to you?"

Herr Rosen is joining us. "Frau Kohn, you remember me, I am Herr Rosen. If I may ask you a few questions, please?"

"I am already in jail, go ahead. At least I don't have to listen to my roommate for a while," she cackles. Yes, she cackles. That's a first, and it's so funny I cackle back.

"Did you know Herr Schumann?"

"Who is he?" She sounds puzzled.

"He was your next-door neighbor. 's stepfather."

"No. Never saw him up close. They were quiet like we, except we screamed between our quiet." And she cackles again.

"He disappeared at about the time your first Rottweiler got shot. He went out into the yard and never came back in."

"No, never heard about it."

"We might have to dig up the yard."

"If you let me out, I'll help you dig, there might be a whole army buried back there," she cackles again, and her face lights up like 'life is great.' She might be cracking up. Herr Rosen thanks her for her time and returns to his seat.

"I am glad to see you happy and well-fed," I say and mean it.

"It was nice when you played the piano. I wanted to play but was too scared to make mistakes. My Father didn't allow mistakes. He was a hard man. But you didn't come to visit me, did you. You can go now. Good-bye."

We were having a conversation, it's shocking! And she was scared to play the piano! Her Father was a bastard, too. I almost pity the old bitch. All her life, she lived with horrible, cruel men.

Back in the car, the two of us are quiet. There isn't much to say. I am curious what kind of father would fault his child so harshly but realize that it is too late for her story. I don't need to know. She destroyed it. But I can't help thinking about her cackling and chatting away. Next time she might sing me a song and tap dance. Herr Rosen drops me off at Frau Graf's house. I enter quietly, take off my shoes and go into the study. She is giving a lesson.

In two days, they will dig up the backyard. I will stay far away that day, maybe visit Frau Rittenmaier. It's time to clear the air with all my good friends, and I miss them suddenly very much, especially Josef and Martina. Maybe I will buy them a toy.

I do have money now. The butcher from town is renting our place and might buy it one day. For now, he and his wife scrubbed and cleaned and repainted the whole building including all my memories. They don't belong there anymore, and I visit with no ill effect. She took off the torn kitchen curtain and replaced it with a new one. The windows are invisible from so much cleaning, and they let in the morning sun. No walls needed to tumble like in Sodom and Gomorra for all the sins that happened in here and I am glad. A lot of paint is all it needed. They transformed the house into a kind and welcoming place, like what happened to me but to a house. Even a house needs love. Outside and along the entry they planted bushes. Being a butcher's wife is not a bad thing if the butcher is nice. Once a week I go to Frau Butcher for a bit of lunch meat and other meats to bring to my three homes, keenly aware of the value of money and how much my friends have done for me.

Maybe sometimes they would have rather been alone. They never let me feel it but always opened their doors and their hearts.

I am nearly done reading 'Oliver Twist.' There are many kids like I am that go through hell and turn out well in the end. It seems to take one good person to show the way. I had three families! How lucky I've been!

Frau Graf's lesson is finished, and I come out of my room. She is saying good-bye to a young man with pimples. He adores her, I can tell. She looks like a movie actress with her red curls pinned up, skin like cream, lips bright red and large green earrings. A piece of vintage furniture if she were a chair.

"Tell me, girl, tell me, how is your Mother, the wicked woman?"

"She quite likes to be in prison, considers it a vacation rather than a punishment. She chatted away and giggled and cackled, looked years younger but couldn't help with the Rottweiler."

"You are quite animated. I think the visit was good for you

as well. Try it again someday. Now let's go to where your Father lies. Get him out of your blood so you can stop your blood curdling howls during the night. I am tired of it."

"How much do you charge for your lessons?"

"Thousands."

"Please, seriously. How much? I earn money now from renting out the store."

"You will need it when you go to college. You can help me out when I am old and feeble, and you feel sorry for me. And now let's go."

She drags me along into town through throngs of people in a hurry to get their shopping done before stores close for the midday meal. The park is crowded with young mothers enjoying a balmy day with their babies. The trees still wear their wintery skeletons, gnarled roots spread on the surface like old people's arthritic fingers. There is a small pond behind the library. Ducks and geese will be back soon. We walk around and enter a small cemetery with large evergreens. To keep the dead in the dark, I guess, or keep them from getting sunburned. I feel silly. It is supposed to be a solemn occasion. Screw the solemn!

"Where is that son of a bitch Father murderer rapist, show me so I can piss on him," I sing with enthusiasm.

"Young girl, that's no way to speak of the dead."

I had no idea there was another living soul besides us. "I am sorry, really sorry. I thought they were all dead."

An old geezer looks at me with slightly bulging eyes.

"Don't worry, I don't like the person I am visiting either." And he gets up and leaves, cackling like Mother.

. . .

Frau Graf shakes her head with amusement as she pulls me a bit further along. "Must be a new thing, people coming here to celebrate. Here, that's him."

She points to a grave with no marker, no flowers and starts to pick weeds along the fence. I wouldn't want flowers for him. Weeds are perfect, dead fibrous stalks. She throws them over the grave. How gently they touch down and spread over where he will rot in eternity! Too gentle. I pick up rocks and throw them at him. He will never get out. By next spring, the weeds will reseed with flowers and it might even look pretty, but I'll never be back, and he'll never be out. Never. And I keep throwing rocks, harder and harder, till a searing emptiness fills me with a nauseating agony, a pain of body and soul. It is an ancient pain, suffered long ago. I sob and moan, go on my knees, rock my body, and my shoulders shake from the sorrow. I hit the ground with my fists. "It is not for you I grieve, you bastard, it is for me," I scream out loud. "For the wounds on my body, the hate and the fear you poisoned me with, ready to crush me at any moment." All the hurt is coming back, and I feel chills in the flames of emotions that twist me like I were a nothing once again. The grief is pulling me flat down onto the frozen ground and nearly into his grave, where he lays dead and moldering, and I convulse and vomit and let my emptiness shatter into frozen pieces of pain.

Time does not exist in such times of grief. One must finish the grieving till the tears have dried and the garbage is out, and our insides are torn to shreds. I am done.

My body and soul are my own again, and I turn my head towards Frau Graf. She reaches down and helps me get up. Her eyes are filled with heart wrenching tears that I've just now come to understand. They are spilling for her own ancient grief and for mine. From now on, my tears will always spill alongside the grief I will feel for others. She puts her arms around me, and we hold on to each other with a desperation I have not known maybe since the day I was stolen.

Slowly, we walk back home, shaken to the core. I know that my life has turned a corner. Herr Rosen is not coming tonight, and we eat leftovers of leftovers, then quietly spend the evening sitting as close together as we can, reading our separate books. Both are upside down. We don't talk, because we don't need to. At bedtime, I say: "thank you," and we hug again.

"I love you too," she cries, and I begin a night without the mares.

24

TO A NEW BEGINNING

I t is today that the police will dig up the back yard. What will they find? How many will they find? I want to watch but must go to school. And I want to go to school and not have to watch since I am still emotionally exhausted from visiting Father's grave. I had hoped to feel lighter afterwards but instead, the grieving has left a heavy residue in me. It weighs me down and makes me sick without being sick, and my steps are tentative like a sailor's coming off a ship. I wonder whether Father will join the other shadows in my life. A tribe of shadow people with one shadow pig.

The right sleeve of my coat is shiny from wiping my nose on it at the graveside. It is dry now and comes off quickly. How easy to rub away outward manifestations of one's sorrow!

After school, I bike to town to buy presents for Frau Rittenmaier and the twins, anxious to visit before they won't like me anymore. I don't know why I feel that way, just that I do. My presents and my visit seem essential and more important than knowing how many bodies they found.

What would they like? I have never bought a gift for anybody, and the stores confuse me with all their choices. I find myself buying meat, more than usual, and some chocolate. A cheesecake would be yummy, but I couldn't carry it on the bike. Most importantly, I would want it for myself, my mouth is watering at the thought, and that might not be considered a present.

The twins see me walk up the path to the entry.

"Mama, she's at the door," they yell.

"Hello, my dear," their Mama shouts, running to me with open arms. My eyes are welling up. We embrace with much care, and I feel as welcomed as I ever was. She has slowly gained some weight over the years and looks matronly now, but even more comforting for it.

"Martina and Josef, how are you, my little ones, I have missed you so much." I hand the meat and the chocolate to Frau Rittenmaier, then stretch out on the floor, grab ahold of them, and we rough house and wrestle and laugh until they have enough and run away. Then they come back and Josef shows me how to draw a house with a train on top of the roof in hopes to make me laugh while Martina draws buildings with arms and legs. And I do laugh, and already, they love me again.

"Frau Rittenmaier," I ask her quietly, "may I take the kids to a store and buy them something they really want? I felt over-whelmed by the choices. You and Herr Rittenmaier are even harder to find a gift for. Please let me do this, please give me an idea. I have money now."

She looks at me, delighted. "Of course, you can take them. You are right, the new store in town has too much variety. But for Herr Rittenmaier and me, there would be no better present than clearing the air. Stay for dinner, spend the night if you want to. Let's talk when the kids are asleep. Or is it still too hard? We can wait, Klara, really, we can."

"Thank you. Talking is fine. But living through it again, I couldn't do it, no, never again." Oh my God! Just the thought.... I start sobbing, and she puts an arm around me.

"Don't let go of me, please hold me hard. Don't let go."

And she holds me with both arms, rocks me and whispers "Never again!"

The twins are rolling around the floor. Their birthday is coming up.

"You were taken at such an early age. I can't imagine how a parent survives such an ordeal."

I stare at her, stare at the kids. If someone took one of them, what would happen to the rest of the family?

"I wonder how long it took my parents to forget about me." I say it and hear how dumb it sounds.

"Klara, crazy girl, your parents never forgot you, there will always be that heart break and a hope. They don't even know if you are dead or alive. Do think about them before it's too late. You used to remember brothers and a sister. They will still miss you. They were older."

"How do you know?"

"You told me they were running while your Mother held you in her arms."

I hear her but can't wrap my heart around it. Not now.

"Today, they are digging up the yard for bodies. I can't think of digging up my real family right now. I saw his grave today. It started out funny." And I tell her about the cemetery and the stranger with the frog eyes.

Then she tells me about her father who died in WWI on the Western Front.

"He was very young. Met my Mama when she was only sixteen. He was eighteen when they sent him off. He left her pregnant, came back for one visit and got her pregnant with my brother. That was the end of Father. They tell everybody their loved ones were heroes but that's of no comfort. He didn't want to go to war and be a hero, and he didn't want to shoot anybody. My brother Ulrich stepped on a mine after the war. He was left in smithereens, fourteen years of age. We were very close. That left me and Mama."

"I never knew, I am so sorry."

"Everybody has suffered great losses after two big wars. Such grief does not go away, but it softens. At least our own personal grief does."

"What do you mean? What other grief is there?"

"Our collective grief as a country. The unspeakable, unbearable atrocities that happened, they will linger forever in our consciousness. But we keep living, learn to enjoy the here and now. The twins and my husband, I treasure every day with them. Ulrich, Ulli we called him, is always by my side like the shadows that you have described of your family." Her eyes are getting misty. "You helped me a great deal, Klara, because I saw your pain and helping you helped me heal as well. I was too young to remember Father, and yet, how often I think about him. He is alive through photos and the many stories my Mother told me."

She is a bit emotional and gets up to get a handkerchief and a photo album from the bookcase to show me the strong resemblance of her and her Father and brother. What does my family look like? Would I have somebody's nose? Would a stranger have my very own webbed toes?

We make a light dinner with bread, cheese and some of the sausages I brought. It's what the kids love above all, and I forced myself to buy them. Their shape still makes me gag from feeling his touch on my nakedness. I toss a green salad with cucumbers even though they, too, look like 'big bad boys.' At least they are green and don't smell of meat.

Martina carries one spoon at a time to the table, and Josef does the same with forks. He makes sure to lick each one of them before use, 'so that they are clean,' he says.

Afterwards, I take care of the dishes while the parents bring the kids to bed with stories and goodnight songs. I was their age when I was taken. How would they survive what I went through? Are my parents still grieving? And what if I found them. Would they be glad or disappointed in me? Why don't they find me?

Yes, there is the problem with my name and age. How can they ever find me?

One more goodnight kiss, one last one, and one very last one, and Herr and Frau Rittenmaier turn off the lights, come out with the door a crack open, and we sit down for our heart to heart talk.

"I love to watch you be parents. How do you know how to do it?" They both answer together.

"Loving them above all, more than anything in the world, laughing and singing together, reading and teaching them. Encourage rather than discourage. And be good role models. After that, a lot of wishful thinking."

"And you never tire of it?"

"Girl," he says, just like Frau Graf, "of course we do. "Getting up at night, cleaning up their mess, watching them kill each other. We are no saints. It's exhausting, annoying, and at the end of the day we want to give them away. Then they fall asleep in their beds, warm and innocent little angels, and miraculously we want to wake them up again for a snuggle."

"Don't you dare," threatens Frau Rittenmaier. "Let's hear about you while they are asleep".

I tell them about that night at Frau Schumann's house, how I howled from fear, and how maybe Father killed her husband also.

"They are just digging up our backyard. Oops. I am not supposed to tell! Please ignore it, I'll tell you what happened as soon as I know."

I tell them about Mother in prison, how much she likes it, that the police should send her back to the butchery for punishment. And I talk about the visit to Father's grave.

"I finally feel safe; there is no way he is getting out. Can you ever forgive me? I owe you for so many years of your love and your help. I can't imagine life without you."

Herr Rittenmaier gets up and sits down next to me. He takes my hand in both of his.

"You needed a kick in the butt, that's all. Nothing to forgive. We'll be lucky if Martina and Josef turn out as well as you." His eyes are moist. He takes off his heavy glasses to wipe his eyes and the glasses, then he scratches his scalp with vigor till it bleeds.

"Thank you. And I still owe you for a new mattress. It was the most embarrassing moment of my life, waking up in a puddle of pee."

"Thank you but no way," he says. I quickly interrupt him:

"Please let me buy you a new one, or maybe two for the twins, they will need larger beds soon. I need to do this. I've been spending money on me, and where's the fun in that? And on Sunday, can you help me explore the mountain behind the park? I've always wanted to see our town from high up. Please. It would mean a lot to me!"

They exchange some glances and nod their heads.

"We'll come with you. But it is not a mountain, just a hill, nothing like the hike you did. Even the kids can come along."

Herr Rittenmaier goes into the kitchen and comes back with a bottle of red wine and a tray with three glasses.

"Let's drink to a new beginning." He pours me less than half a glass. Little do I know what it can do to a girl with an almost empty and seriously fermenting stomach. The alcohol seeps into my arms and legs, a warming, loving ambrosia that loosens my limbs. I say good night and leave while I can.

25

THE WONDERS OF WINE

S lightly inebriated, I try riding my bicycle with a body that flops and flounders like a hot potato. It might not be mine. And my brain is loose and liberated, and it seesaws against the rhythm of my body. It's tricky to pedal back to Frau Graf. I nearly fall in a ditch, and it's hilarious, and I swear to drink more from now on or less. Not sure which one. Less and forth, back or more... I shout it into the night on top of my voice.

"Frau Graf," I say, when she opens the door even before I knock. "I am so crappy to know you."

"You are drunk! I heard you from two streets over."

"No, I am crappy. My body's floating, so crappy...." my body moves like a ballerina or a monkey, and she grabs me and takes me to bed.

"Go sleep. I'll tell you tomorrow what else they found in the back yard besides bodies."

"Tell me less or not...?"

"Lie down first," she says, and I do and wake up the next morning with my clothes on and terrible breath. My head hurts when I move. I am lethargic and decide to drink less from now on. I slowly walk to the kitchen, curious to hear the news and to get a cup of coffee for my headache.

"You smell like hell, and I won't tell you a thing till you are washed and dressed in clean clothes." I stand stock still like a broom, probably look like one, too.

"Moving hurts."

"It's called a hangover. Get over it, hurry, it's almost time for school."

I hurry like a turtle, and when I smell good enough and wear clean clothes, she tells me 'time to leave,' handing me my bread with butter for the morning recess. I'll have to spend all day at school sitting on pins and needles not knowing what and who has been rotting in our back yard.

"How many bodies? Can you give me a number? You are killing me."

"Three. Go!"

When school lets out, I pedal towards my old house. My head still aches. Maybe that's why it's called a headache. Two police cars are parked outside, and a third car belonging to Herr Rosen. I wonder if they are still digging and peek around the corner. Four people are digging in a wide area, Herr Rosen and a police officer looking on. Monika waves to me from her house, and I hope she won't come here and ask questions. What would I say? They found an extra body? Most likely your stepdad? I wave back and leave quickly before she might come over.

On the way to Frau Graf, I pick up some extra meat for tonight, like a celebration. I hold it in one hand and drive with the other. The cold meat feels like Father's flesh, and I almost drop it. What would we be celebrating? An extra corpse? It will be a terribly sad occasion for Monika and her Mother, and I put the meat into the pantry for tomorrow.

Frau Graf has no other news. We set the table, and then she gives me an unexpected piano lesson to make the time go by faster. She works me hard with a Chopin Nocturne and a piece by Mendelssohn, simple sounding but treacherous. It's been one and a half hours already when Herr Rosen finally shows up. He looks seriously distraught and his eyes are red from fatigue. We reheat the meal for all of us and sit down. Nobody talks and only Frau Graf and I eat a bite.

"Fucking bastard," he says finally. "Barely in the grave, still a bastard." He lowers his head into his hands and his shoulders start shaking. He is sobbing. Frau Graf gets up and puts her arms around him and holds him. Her head rests on his shoulder, her nose nestling in his neck, breathing him in. Slowly, he moves his arms around her and pulls her on his lap where they hold each other, his sobs and heaving shoulders the only sound and movement. He makes me sad, and I cry, too. I didn't know how much he means to me.

The big round clock above the piano shows 6:37. Might as well do my journal and homework and go to bed. Herr Rosen and Frau Graf go to their room almost right after me.

There is a new painting on the wall. It is of a café, the night sky lit up with stars. It is a Van Gogh, and I am touched by it and by Frau Graf who is trying to make the little study a bit nicer for me. I take out my journal, look at it and put it back. It needs no other words. What I wrote is enough about the past. It's the future that needs thinking about.

26

WHO ELSE IS BURIED IN THE YARD?

A heavy wind wakes me up. The wooden shutters outside rattle like old bones. It is early, the sun barely reaches over the horizon and the night is clinging to the shadows of trees. My heavy feather blanket is smothering me in a warm and safe snuggle. Random thoughts and random trips to exotic countries rush through my mind in split seconds. Finding my birth family would be a trip like none other. Should I start looking? What keeps me from searching for them right now? What is it that still holds me back?

The sun has claimed what's hers and I get up to make coffee, wanting its smell to welcome Herr Rosen and Frau Graf after their tough night. Then I quickly run to the bakery and buy fresh buns.

"What a treat." They thank me when I come back. Herr Rosen in his blue and white striped pajamas and his dark uncombed hair looks like a sad little boy. He is pale and slouches. I feel strangely honored that he shows himself to me without his usual elegance and strength. He is as vulnerable as all of us, but only we, his family, know. Frau Graf wears a long nightgown. Its flowery design with lace around the neck mellows her. They are my family, together with the other two. Would I have enough love left for my real family? And why am I looking for excuses?

I an unexpected attack of love, I go and hug Herr Rosen. Hug him with all my love for the sadness he had last night.

"Will you tell me your story? I suddenly can't wait to hear it. More so than what you dug up in the yard yesterday."

"Thank you for asking. You could tell last night, couldn't you, how much grief is still stuck inside of me. You got most of yours out. Frau Graf told me about your unconventional visit to the cemetery."

"Yeah. Grief and anger are heavy like a cow's carcass. Sorry to talk like a butcher's daughter, but I've been around dead meat all my life; it's normal. I had no nightmare last night, must have cried it up and out and good-bye."

"Up and out and good-bye, maybe it will work for me, too. Let me quickly tell you what happened yesterday, and the next available evening we can talk about Frau Graf and me. There will be lots of up and out and good-byes. I feel the weight of several oxen."

We sit down and enjoy a loving but subdued breakfast together.

"About yesterday. We dug up what seems to be Herr Schumann. Frau Schumann identified him by the shoes that were still recognizable. It was a tremendous shock to her, but at least she and Monika know he didn't abandon them. He was shot from the back. I don't know if there is a silver lining in it. It was shocking. Herr Rittenmaier volunteered to stay with them last night. He is awfully kind. I couldn't have done it. We also found what seems to be the body of Hans and the little girl. All bodies were simply thrown into the dirt. Not far from them was a metal container without a key. We sent it to police headquarters for opening along with the remains of Herr Schumann to see if there were bite marks on his body besides the gun shot. We should know what they find by next week. There were no remains from the Rottweiler. We checked the whole area where the ground is soft."

"What if Father ground him up for meat?" I feel sick at the thought.

Herr Rosen shrugs his shoulders. "He wouldn't be the first butcher. And it wouldn't be tragic. I bet the lamppost caught stray dogs and brought them to Father. Dog meat is not dangerous. Others have even used human flesh during times of hunger, or for other reasons."

"Could you find out, please?" I am suddenly anxious to know.

"You must be joking! We ate so many of your sausages and so did the Dietrichs and the Rittenmaiers. Don't get your knickers in a twist over it. We survived."

"What if they would like to know?"

"They would not; trust me."

Frau Graf is watching me like a hawk. "Get your mind off it, girl. We ate what we ate. Swallow it! It has long since been flushed down and out. Now off you go, and after school we could visit Frau Schumann and Monika, you and I."

. . .

Another day at school. I am tired of it and glad it will be over soon. I am still deeply embarrassed when coming across the boys that went to the park with me. We keep trying hard to avoid each other. Today's lesson is about Napoleon and Bismarck. It seems wrong. Now should only be about now.

There is Harald coming around a corner. I walk straight up to him to apologize, tell him how much sick stuff has happened to me lately, and that I am glad he and Isabel found each other, "but I am still a bit jealous," I say, and he gives me a nice smile, sad and glad, and we shake hands or rather, we don't shake them, just hold on for a while, warm and forgiving.

After school Frau Graf and I eat a quick midday meal of Frikadellen – ground beef patties made with parsley, eggs, breadcrumbs and onion, and yes, the meat is from the new butcher, there is none left from our store, - dog, cow or human - before visiting Frau Schumann. The sun is shining, not a cloud in sight, and we walk arm in arm. Her steps are longer than mine, and I try to keep up. I am bringing the piece of meat I bought yesterday as a present, hoping she will appreciate it. Frau Graf thinks she will for sure.

Monika opens the door before we even knock.

"Please come in, have a seat. I am so glad you came."

Frau Schumann comes out of her room, her face swollen from crying. She, too, seems to be happy to see us, and we shake hands for longer than usual.

"Klara, we admire you for linking my husband's disappearance to your Rottweiler. It has been such a long time living with this wound. It kept festering you know. How can I ever thank you enough?" She throws her arms around me. "Thank you, thank you, thank you so much."

"We never got over it. Mama had a wonderful man wanting to marry her and be my stepdad. I liked him too. But it was too hard at the time. We worried he might leave us too. I am so grateful to you, maybe the same way you felt when you heard my name. I get it now."

Frau Schumann is making tea for us and I go to the kitchen and give her the meat.

"It's a strange gift, it seemed entirely wrong, but chocolate or flowers seemed more wrong," I explain.

"Meat is wonderful. We don't eat enough of it, and if you would like, you may eat with us."

"I have a piano lesson to give in a short time," says Frau Graf. "But we can have dinner another day. I would like it." And I add that I would like it also and will bring more meat to share.

Frau Graf looks at the photos of the three of them, at the love that pours out of the frame.

"You never really believed he just up and left. You would have taken those photos down long ago," she says. "I am happy for you that you were right."

We sit down and drink our tea. After a long thoughtful pause Frau Schumann responds.

"You are right, Frau Graf, I never could believe he would simply leave, but I had to. And still, I couldn't because I felt that he didn't. My mind and my heart were of different opinions, and it tore me to pieces."

With that we take our leave and walk back home. Out of the blue, I tell her about Father and what he did. It is easy and not at all shameful, even with all the details. Her first reaction surprises me.

"I hope you'll start eating sausages again." How did she know?

"We all noticed that you didn't touch them. Your face would gag from disgust. It was obvious what it was about."

That's what it boils down to. Sausages gave me away. Ach!

"Girl, getting that out of you was like giving birth to a baby your Father's size. It doesn't sound like he had time to finish the job, but have you had your period since?"

"Yes, right now." We almost want to laugh from relief, but I doubt it will ever turn into a laughing matter.

Halfway to Frau Graf we part ways. She to give her lesson, I to go to the Rittenmaier's to take them shopping. He is catching up on the sleep he missed last night at the Schumann's house, and only Frau Rittenmaier and the twins come along. There is a new store in town with catalogues. We fill out an order form, and in six weeks, two mattresses will show up at the doorstep. It's the newest craze! On the way home, we stop at the toy store to buy little bicycles. One for Josef and one for Martina. It won't take long, or so I think.

Holy Moses, son of someone! She wants red, so he wants red, so she wants green, then he wants green. Then they cry. Now he wants yellow, and she wants red again. We leave with two blue bikes. On the way, I pick up a fresh yeast cake with streusel on top. Herr Rittenmaier just got up, still wears his pajamas, ravenous after the long night with Frau Schumann and Monika. He stares at the cake with hungry eyes, and I hand it to him.

"Pig out if you want to."

He digs in with his hand, pulls off a piece and stuffs his mouth. Streusel gets stuck on his unshaven chin and falls on the ground. Another pig, I respect him for it! But he does need a haircut even with hardly any hair. At what point will he cut it himself? Would he pay for having ten hairs cut? I believe, once you can figure out the price per hair you should cut it yourself. But I don't tell him because my manners are nearly perfect now. Then I go back to Frau Graf.

"Guess what was in the metal container," asks Herr Rosen as soon as he comes home.

"Gold and Silver," guesses Frau Graf, and he nods.

"Mostly gold, probably from all those murdered people's teeth, and lots of jewelry. Worth a fortune. I wonder how they stole it, who the mastermind was. My bet is the chief of police. The scarecrow stole it, the chief used his brain to get it out and hide it. I need to take another trip to prison. Would be nice if it were the last time! I am so tired to see their lying stupid faces."

"Tomorrow the Rittenmaiers and I plan to hike up the hill behind the park. Would you like to come along?"

They look at each other.

"I could use a rest, read a book," he says.

"Me, too, put my legs up," says she.

"Let's go then." Those two have the strangest conversations.

"And tomorrow night, when we get back dead tired, you tell me the end of your story, Frau Graf, and you Herr Rosen, everything about your life, because I know nothing about it, and you know everything about mine."

"It's a short hike up the hill, more like a walk. You will not see the world from up there. We could do it five times in a row and still smell like a rose," warns Herr Rosen.

"You will certainly not hear the music of the universe or of the university, because both are too far away," jokes Frau Graf.

"Just tell me your darn story, darnit, whenever."

27

STORY OF HERR ROSEN AND
FRAU GRAF

The day for our walk up the small hill is of the bluest, most sparkling sunshine. It is almost springtime. The first crocuses in purple peek out through patches of snow, and snowbells are everywhere. What looked like dead wood a week ago is wearing a faint touch of color, the first juice of life. We meet Herr and Frau Rittenmaier with the twins at the foot of the hill. It is a small hill, but it stretches out far enough to call it a good outing. Most of the town's people had the same idea, and the little hill is turning into a regular anthill. It is amusing to observe the end of hibernation with hundreds of curtseys and handshakes up and down the hill. Martina is practicing her little curtseys for anybody she sees, even for dogs. Josef bows his head like his Father but many times up and down and up and sideways. And everybody says: 'Good day.'

I grab the twin's hands, and we start skipping to introduce a new rhythm into this slow movement of humans, and we sing from the top of our lungs. It frees me from the crowd and from their looks of benign curiosity and their whispers of 'poor girl, she's the one.'

The view at the top of the hill is serene, peaceful. Nothing like the humbling, antlike experience on the high mountain which so clearly pointed out my insignificance. I will never forget it. When people call me gifted, I will remain humble. I've always done much thinking because that's all I ever had. Thoughts were my toys. Take a thought, turn it left, turn it right and upside down, inside out, then watch it emerge in different shapes and colors. Mostly the color red for all the blood in my life. But my true gifts are my families. Where would I be without them? In an early grave? A somber thought.

Back down, we go our separate ways. The Rittenmaiers carry their tired and cranky twins for the midday meal and a nap. Then they plan on teaching them how to ride their bikes. And I can't wait to finally hear the story of Frau Graf and Herr Rosen.

"But first" he says, "let's stop for some coffee and cake."

There is a small bakery on the way where we each order a cup of coffee and a slice of cake. Plum cake with whipped cream for them, cheesecake for me.

"Kids are nice," I say, "and then I want to hand them back. Is that bad?"

"Think of it when you go out with boys. Don't get pregnant, you can't hand them back," says Frau Graf.

I give her my evil eye. The people next to us heard every word and noticeably perked up from their own boring life. I whisper:

"I tell every boy I go out with that I don't want to get pregnant."

"Tell her, Herr Rosen. Enlighten her." Her voice is entirely too loud, as is his!

"Boys don't get pregnant. Frankly, until they are older and wiser, like my age, they don't care about you because the only brains are in their pants. They'll say: 'I love you,' and 'I can't live without you.' It's all lies! In other words, you alone are responsible to not let it happen."

"Oh darn! What a sad life. I'll stick with cheesecake then, for now. But promise to buy it for me most every day."

"Sorry, I'd get fat and Herr Rosen might look for another woman."

"I do look at other women, but you are the only one I ever want. If you get fat, I will love your fat."

Back at the house, we take off our warm clothes and sit down. The two love birds take the sofa, and I snuggle into an easy chair. There is another new painting on the wall. It has broad brush strokes and striking colors, and people that look brown and luscious.

"It's a Gauguin, a French man who moved to Polynesia to paint," explains Herr Rosen. "He describes the lives of the natives through paint, without a single word. It amazes me."

"Can you tell me the story of your life through words without a single drop of paint, please? Like right now?"

He looks at Frau Graf. "Where shall we begin?"

"I told her how we met on the cliff above the lake. You heard my screams, you looked around a rock, and I fell head over heels into love and into the water."

"And I jumped after you to save what seemed most precious; your red curls and green swollen eyes from crying and screaming. Those got me hooked like a fish."

"We were freezing. Herr Rosen looked like an icicle with

his skinny frame while I sheltered inside my voluptuous body. We wrung out our wet stuff. He peeked at my nakedness and warmed up to it. I saw it while peeking at him. Then we ran back up to our back packs where we had extra sweaters. The sheer amount of exertion we needed for climbing the devilish steep hill next to the lake kept us not warm but enough to stay alive. Then we ran as quickly as possible before catching pneumonia."

Herr Rosen is looking right into her story, with that faraway look that leaves only him and Frau Graf. I am a piece of disposable furniture during those moments.

"Frau Graf," he says, "you are a woman with stamina. When I thought of collapsing, you kept me going with promises of things we might do later, naughty girl. At times, I expected you to pick me up and carry me. But you didn't. That was my first disappointment in you."

"What was the second one?" She whispers.

"I am still waiting for it. You are all I want, you know that." His elegant, long fingered hands are sitting very still on his knees. He looks at her as if waiting for some answer. She fiddles with one of her curls like a little schoolgirl.

How old are you?" I ask. "You suddenly seem like two young high school sweethearts."

"I am 37 years old, and Frau Graf will be 36 in a few days."

"Wow! And you are still flirting. Gross! How old do you think Mother is, the old hag?"

"About mid-forties."

"No! What are you saying? I thought she might be seventy."

"Great hardships do that to a person," says Herr Rosen.

"Then the two of you must have had an easy life."

"You decide. We were lucky to find a barn before too long. It was warm from cows and their steaming manure, a tad smelly for us city folks. We spent the night there. It took hours before we stopped shivering. Our coats kind of dried, enough to wear them for the long hike back, around twenty more kilometers. During the night in the barn, I told Frau Graf my story. I was from a well-known Jewish family and very scared for our lives. That's why I went on this long hike, to figure out what to do, where to go.

When we got close to town, we waited for darkness. I was way too Jewish looking, and lots of people knew me. Maybe some would have helped, but maybe not. In times like that you don't know which friends are your real friends. And even those might be too scared. Frau Graf put her hat on my head to hide my black hair and draped her scarf around my face. When people walked by, I got jittery, and Frau Graf kissed me. By God, she kissed me. I was the happiest jittery man scared for his life to ever walk the streets. We walked all the way close to where I lived. There were no lights inside our house. There were no sounds. I didn't dare enter. Instead, we walked a bit further where good friends of my family lived, Jewish also. We were met with the same eerie quiet and darkness."

"I left Herr Rosen in a dark corner and asked an older couple on the street what happened to that family. 'All taken away, as were the other families in this neighborhood,' they told me. 'They were good people.' And I had to go back and tell Herr Rosen."

"We collapsed into each other's arms and cried us a tub full of tears. Cried and walked for hours through the night, away from streetlights, to Frau Graf's one-bedroom apartment. She smuggled me in on tip toes and kept me hidden for close to three weeks. It was hard. I couldn't go near the window, couldn't make any noise when she was not home, even a hard cough might have given me away. We were afraid of pneumonia from the day we almost froze. A good thing she had her own bathroom, which of course I could not flush till she came home."

"We were lucky," continues Frau Graf. I had made good friends at the University, friends I could trust. We had many conversations about what was happening in Germany, and we all wished we could help. Some knew of organizations that smuggled Jews out of the country. Meanwhile, I had to find food for him, and I couldn't just shop twice as much as I was known to buy. There were spies everywhere."

"One evening, somebody knocked at the door. I hid under the bed the way we had practiced, and then stopped breathing. But it wasn't the Gestapo, the Secret Police, it was a woman who came to take me away. I had to come right now, she said, and she could tell nothing else. There was no good-bye, no hug, no kiss. 'Come,' and we left without a sound, our footsteps synchronized as one person. If ever I was close to shitting my pants, this was it. On top of leaving Frau Graf, the love of my life, I felt an insane grief for my family. Did anyone get away? Will I get away? And where to?

A car was waiting with the engine running. I sat in the back. Someone put a light brown wig on me and a hat. The next days were spend hiding during the day, driving at night or walking, at times running when we heard dogs, until we got to a boat, hungry, frightened and cold to the bone. Four of us were joined by ten others. It was a long, hazardous journey, and I don't care to describe it. Eight died. Six made it to Israel."

. . .

"How big was your family?"

"I had parents. They were good people, but we didn't get along. They were orthodox and wanted me to be a scholar and marry the daughter of a rabbi. I wanted neither. They were angry at me, because they had promised him that I would marry her. Then there were three brothers, two of them very religious also, and I loved them but had no patience for their thinking. The other one, a bit older than I, studied engineering, and my younger sister studied to be a nurse. The three of us were very close and we supported each other in our worldly choices. I studied history and literature and wanted to be a writer."

"And with that, he was gone," continues Frau Graf. The emptiness is impossible to describe because of the fear that went with it. I could do nothing but wait in a total vacuum. Was he alive, the love of my life? Was he injured, was he caught, did he suffer?" I missed one semester, sick from grief and worry, and from morning sickness. Yes, I was pregnant. What should have been such a glorious time turned into pure agony. Carrying his child, not knowing what to do about it. You couldn't have a baby being unmarried. And I wanted it, especially if Herr Rosen had not survived. Mother was my only family. I couldn't possibly burden her with an illegitimate baby, so I gave her up for adoption, an open adoption so she could find me one day. She would be about your age. But she hasn't found me yet. She is stubborn like you."

. . .

"I stayed in Israel till the war ended; had no way to let Frau Graf know that I lived. I did find my sister Lilly in Israel, and we are looking for our brothers. We are quite sure from witnesses that our parents are gone as well as my two oldest brothers. They didn't have the fight in them, trusting too much in their God."

"And that, my dear, is our story," finishes Frau Graf. Both look glassy eyed and so very lost. "Now you understand one of our reasons for loving you. You could be our daughter. She would be about your age and at least as smart and beautiful. She had my curly red hair."

Herr Rosen's elegant hands are balled into fists. "Maybe you finally understand why we push you to look for your real parents. Somebody out there misses you terribly, and we hope you will start to feel the urgency. If not for you, then do it for them. Do it now." Herr Rosen is close to yelling at me.

28

DUMB SCUM

"You'd think if they were smart, they'd point the finger at the butcher for stealing the gold and killing Herr Schumann. He is dead and can't deny it. They'd be off the hook. But no, the police chief knows nothing. He squirms and squiggles and sweats like a pig from his lies."

Herr Rosen is noticeably trembling. He just returned from prison where he interviewed the chief of police again and the lamppost.

"The scarecrow freely admits to the torturing, raping and killing of men, women and children with not a hint of guilt. One more crime would be a matter of pride to him. But he fervently defends himself against theft. 'Being labeled a thief might give me a bad reputation,' he said. He is sicker than I thought, and I believe him. He insists he did not shoot the butcher, says 'I liked Fritz. We are both scum like soulmates.' Then he said 'the police chief, the son of a bitch, he was full of shit. Thought his smelled better than ours. If it were him dead, I probably would have been the one who'd done it. But not Fritz, my friend.'

. . .

He didn't know the neighbor guy, Herr Schumann, and knew nothing about him. Well, we have enough on both to put them away for good. We got the result from the remains of the bones. Herr Schumann had bite marks consistent with a large dog and got shot in the back of the head. I am sure it was the chief, who else has a gun? He and Fritz stole the gold, but the police chief wanted it for himself. He probably made plans to get his butt to South America to join so many other Nazis. Good riddance to them both. The world will be a better place, amen and hallelujah."

"I can't believe the lamppost called himself a soulmate to Father; it's obscene. They didn't have souls. It bothers me."

"Call them shit mates if it feels better. Don't let things like that bother you, Klara. They are dead now or rotting behind bars."

Frau Graf is right, of course.

"Do you think I am emotionally crippled?" I wonder.

"We all are, you are not special that way. Look at the men that had their arms and legs blown off and the soldiers, the things they did, the things they saw."

"Herr Rosen, did the lamppost know you are Jewish? How could he look you in the eyes after what he did?"

"He is a psychopath, not a racist. He couldn't care less what I am. I believe every psychopath in Germany got a job under Hitler. They were able to do legitimately what otherwise would have been criminal."

"We should probably tell you that we started to look for relatives of your fake Mother, just so you know," continues Frau Graf and changing the subject.

"Why would you do that? They would hate what she's become."

"Think about Frau Schumann. The truth about her husband stirred up the old wound, but now it can heal. Your fake Mother's family might still be looking. If they find her and hate her, they can live with it. And one day, when your family sees you for the first time, those shadow legs that you remember running away will run towards you in the flesh and blood. They'll grab you wherever there's space, and they will shout 'sweetest girl.' And you will love it."

"Oh, Frau Graf. If they are all like you, so full of passion, they will eat me alive."

"I hope they will," she answers. "Until that day, you will stay with us. This is your home now, and we will even get a few more paintings for the study. We believe, Herr Rosen and I, that your family has great artistic talent."

Herr Rosen is thinking. He sits with his chin nesting in his palm, fingers stretched over his cheek. He even took off his glasses.

"You are so talented we might keep you. We could send our own daughter, if she contacts us, to your parents. A fair and easy trade, nobody will know, everybody will be happy."

"Not even funny," growls Frau Graf.

29

KLARA'S FIRST LOVER

y life has been so peaceful that my grades are back to perfection and my thoughts are so boring I could talk about them without shame; which by itself is shameful at my age. But I took Frau Graf's advice to heart. If I want to find my passion, I can't go out and get pregnant by a handsome face and a hot body. Why is it so awfully hard? If God exists, why does he want us to make babies when we are still kids? He should require some kind of a copulation license. Yes, my thoughts do wander a lot.

Instead of boys, I take more bike rides. And today, something happened to me when I rode my bike through the park. It was cloudy. Very noisy birds bustled about like they owned it, and I was the intruder. It felt good sitting on the bike, really good, more so than usual. I kept pedaling, and as I pedaled along, I realized that the good feeling was right where I was sitting on the seat. I kept going and going in circles since the park is quite small, and it felt better and better, like it's about to boil over. I stopped in time for a fiery earthquake in my privates. I got off the bike and held very still, listening to my body. What just happened? I did not know, only that it was very good. I sat down on a bench. Will there be more of those, I wondered? And does it have a name? I am sure it had to do with boys but without a boy.

Tonight, before Herr Rosen comes, I tell Frau Graf about it.

"Frau Graf, while riding my bike, I had what felt like an earthquake in my privates. And I wet my pants a bit. Do you know what that might have been?"

"Girl," she says, "that was an orgasm, you lucky thing. See, you don't even need a boy. A good bike is all you need. Herr Rosen, our girl had an orgasm," she yells before even greeting him. He just entered the room, takes off his hat, a bit embarrassed by her enthusiasm, I believe, since he lingers, looks in the mirror, and then he empties his pockets. He never empties them. He always leaves this wallet, a handkerchief and a key for the next day. Then he turns around quite slowly.

"Frau Graf. What's the matter with you! Certain things are private. But it is a wonderful thing to have an orgasm. Congratulations, Klara." And he looks right at me and my beet red face and says: "It's like having a birthday, and we wish you many more. Now let's eat."

"You mean, it happens only once a year?" They are laughing their heads off.

"It's one of our few God given pleasures that doesn't cost a thing, like laughing or singing. Use it!!!" She says.

"Unless you want to be a whore who gets paid or a nun who gets neither," he adds. "Both are undesirable."

We eat our simple evening meal. A salad made just with greens, some leftover pieces of liver with fried potatoes, and freshly buttered pretzels. I already feel that I want more of this God given pleasure since all it takes is to think of Harald. But I don't want them or anybody else to know. It is too embarrassing, and he and Isabel are firmly in love.

"Girl, don't be embarrassed. You are thinking about it right now, I can tell. It's normal. Ask if you have more questions," says Frau Graf.

"I need to get out of here and cool off. It's too hot in here with you two," I sigh.

"We'll join you." He is already putting on his hat. He needs fresh air as well. Frau Graf has that effect.

"Promise to keep my private stuff private, please! Nobody else needs to know what happened to me on my bike."

"It happened on your bike? Girl, your rusty old bike was your first lover? I hope you find better ones one day, or get a better bike," laughs Herr Rosen, and I could strangle him and her. But I giggle because it is funny.

30

THE GHOST OF FATHER AND A CONCERT

Seldom do I look back to the years at the butcher's house, and when I walk by the building it seems strangely foreign to me, like it never happened. I seldom dream of Mother, but strangely it is Father who sometimes enters my mind, surprising me with a certain playfulness. He will chase me down a hallway laughing, not angry and without the cleaver dripping with blood. Did he ever try to play with me? Did I piss him off because I screamed from fear when he felt friendly? Could I have tried to smile at him, at least once? I hated him from the moment we met. Maybe if I had tried, he would have been nicer to Mother, and she would have been nicer to both. I don't know, doesn't matter really, but maybe I'll ask Mother about it one day. Haven't seen her since that first visit.

Maybe I should visit her tomorrow. I would be glad not to hate anybody. But liking her or him? Feeling guilty? That is simply wrong.

. . .

After school, Isabel and I pedal to her house. I visit them often. When Harald shows up and they go out, I feel a touch of nostalgia but know that my life will take a different path. Nicholas is taking piano lessons from me and his weekly progress is amazing.

"Without your fake family there is nothing scary going on," complains Herr Dietrich. "Without you, this town is dying of boredom."

Isabel and I have become like sisters. We gossip and comfortably share our thoughts. Today, I tell her about Father intruding into my dreams as a good guy who makes me feel guilty for hating him.

"No way. Klara, that is sick, you're sick. It's not your Father, it's your real father coming into your mind. You still haven't tried to find them?" I shake my head.

"Well, do it! Are you waiting for them to die? How cruel. Think of their feelings, their memories of you. You have all but forgotten them, but they haven't. They were older. Be kind, Klara, be kind to them! They gave you the love and strength to survive all these years."

I hear her, loud and clear, and with sudden panic, I run home.

"Frau Graf, I want to start looking. What do I need to do? Can I start today?" Goose bumps are running down my spine at the thought.

"Start what?"

"Start looking for my family. I feel their pain. If we don't go, I'll get sick. The butcher is coming back and I feel kindness towards him." She stares at me.

"That is a most troubling thought. I shall take you to the Red Cross next week. It's time to check on my daughter again."

"Next week might be too late. Can you take me now?" I am fidgety and jumpy. She has two more piano lessons to give, and then the office will be closed. I will skip school, and she'll take me first thing in the morning. She understands.

I toss and turn all night. Strangers enter my dream. I recognize the shadows, the running legs, the bloody shoulder. But they are not running away, they are pulling me, unknown and faceless.

I wake up restless and jittery. Wash my face and brush my hair longer than usual and dress into fresh clothes even though it is only Wednesday.

"You look nice."

"We are still going to the Red Cross, aren't we?"

"We sure are. Herr Rosen is coming along to drag you by force, if necessary."

"I am a wreck. Look how shaky I am." I brush my hair again and look in the mirror. I never look in mirrors and hardly look familiar to myself.

"Are you admiring yourself again?"

"No. Just looking. I know me hardly at all. Do you think I am pretty?"

"You are pretty enough." She stands behind me. "You have a nice face, look at it, yes, you are very pretty, and very smart, it's good to know that about yourself, and your nose is in the middle, but then, forget about it, or it becomes a distraction. Is that clear?"

I nod my head, and then we leave. Herr Rosen is waiting for us in the car. During the trip, we are quiet, solemn, each of us imagining our own earth-shattering family reunion.

. . .

The office is quite empty. Most people found their families by now. There is a nice old lady, hair newly rinsed with blue to get the yellow out. It makes no sense.

"Which one of you is looking?" She has a friendly voice.

"This young lady is searching for her family." Herr Rosen is pointing at me. "Afterwards, the rest of us need to follow up on our lost ones."

The lady asks for my information, writes down the details, and disappears for about 25 minutes.

"Sorry it took so long. I checked the whole registry and could not find anything."

Now what? Am I too late, and they died? Or don't they want me? Tears are streaming down my cheeks uncontrollably and Herr Rosen puts his arm around me.

"Don't give up. We'll help you find them."

Frau Graf and Herr Rosen are next in line, giving their daughter's birthdate. How often they've been standing here wishing to hear from her, each time full of hope but trying not to get disappointed. Yet again, there is nothing new. Herr Rosen, however, has a mysterious lady trying to contact HIM from England. He does not know her name. His brother who lives in England, why did he not try to make contact himself? Herr Rosen is worried.

On the spur of the moment, I ask if anybody has contacted them for Rachael Kohn. The lady takes down Mother's name and goes back to the archives.

She comes back very quickly, a big smile on her face. "Somebody is looking for her. A young man in England by the name of Uri Kohn. We will get in touch with him and let him know about Rachael. Where can he find her?"

"She is in prison right here in town."

"The name rings a bell. You are the butcher's daughter? It

was all over the news. What an awful story. For a few days, I loved my kids and grandkids more than ever because of it."

Afterwards, we stop at Herr Rosen's house for the midday meal of a leftover vegetable soup. It was not good when it was fresh and still isn't. Our mood is somber. What else can we do? Maybe advertise in a major newspaper? Frau Graf thinks highly of the Red Cross but believes the chances for mistakes are overwhelming.

"I looked at the ledger. Hand-written notes attached with tape that comes lose, ink bleached and with coffee spills, and human error, it's a huge problem."

Herr Rosen still wonders why a lady is inquiring after him. He twitches his nose, worried. Is his brother sick or did he die? What else could it be?

I think how unfair that somebody is searching for my horrible Mother and nobody for me.

Herr Rosen takes his hat. "I'll see you tonight." And he leaves, his hat on crooked, and I worry about him.

There is still an hour left at school, but I can't go. The sudden hope of finding my family was like a hot fire that turned to cold ashes within seconds. Why did I wait so long? And what can I do? For sure, I don't want to visit Mother now. We go home, utterly deflated. Frau Graf stares into space, then reads the newspaper. Something is catching her eye.

"Let's go to a concert in the big city. A lady pianist, a Frau Zimmermann, is playing a wonderful program. You'll recognize some pieces, but she'll play them way better than I can."

It gives us something to look forward to, but not much. We

don't even smile about it, and it won't happen for another few days.

Then, two events happen, one after the other, with shockwaves that will stay with me for the rest of my life. The lady at the Red Cross remembered me and my story and did some more checking on her own. She came across an old entry where a family is looking for a little girl, four years old with green eyes and a scar across her right leg in the shape of the corner of a table. The birthdate is interesting. It was in autumn that Mother stole me, and I must have just turned four. That's why I always remembered how to show my age; one hand minus the middle finger. Sounds like an older brother taught me.

She notifies us, and we immediately head back to the Red Cross. All the people in the office come to see my leg. They hope for a happy ending, and I slowly lower my right stocking. Here it is, the scar, big and white. I never noticed it before. I only ever noticed my grown together toes, and I nearly faint. My family, they were right here in the ledger. I hold on to Frau Graf, squeeze her arm till she screams. Mostly, who are they and will they love me? Will I love them back?

"We will contact your family at once. If there is a telephone number, they will hear from us today, otherwise it will take a week to ten days. Then we will set up a meeting in this office to verify that you are related."

I am a basket case. Don't know what to feel, what to think or what to do. I hear things that aren't and see stuff that isn't. I don't know what to eat, won't touch the cheesecake that Herr Rosen brings home to celebrate. But I poke a finger in, make a deep hole. I skip school. Go for a walk up the hill instead. Then run down and do it again, all the while without any thoughts. I am terribly, terribly nervous. And I am numb.

Tomorrow is the concert, and I tell Frau Graf I won't be able to listen to the music.

"I'll be too fidgety," I say, but she and Herr Rosen won't hear of it. They drag me to the car and into the concert hall, then they put me between them so I can't get away.

The lady pianist enters to a very friendly welcome, and she bows and looks at us with her blue eyes and greying hair. She has a nice smile, but a sad one. As soon as she sits down and starts playing, I am glad to have come along. She is very good, plays the way I would love to play, and I feel strangely connected to her. At the end of the concert she stands up and talks.

"For many years, I have played one extra piece at the end of my concerts, a Waltz by Brahms. My little girl, Monika, loved it before she got stolen in Berlin, 1944. I always hoped that one day she would hear me and recognize it." She looks around for a second, then adds "if you do, please come to me." With that, she sits back down and starts playing.

I turn into one huge goose bump. It starts in my stomach and spreads to all my limbs. I feel inebriated, cry and laugh. The piece, long forgotten, rattles something in me, in my heart or in my memory, and I shiver and shake, climb over Frau Graf, climb over everybody else, run around chairs and down the aisle, my head grown to twice its size, and I fly onto the stage to the piano and stare at her, heavy teardrops stuck to my eyes and lashes, and she stops playing. I know she is my Mother, my very own real Mother, and she knows it too.

"Your eyes," she says with the softest voice, "like your Father's."

I pull down my stockings, pull them off all the way to show her my toes, and she says: "Your toes, like your Father's," her voice breaking.

And with that, we fall into each other's arms, and neither of us wants to ever let go. We hear nothing of the applause, the yells and shouts of excitement that grab the audience. We are alone, and we don't want to wake up from the dream in case that's all it is. We hold on and hold each other up till a balding man rushes on stage and holds us also. He smells of an oil that I recognize from before my time. Then Herr Rosen and Frau Graf join us, and without words they tightly wrap their arms around Mother, Father and me. They all cry together for their own and each other's sorrows, for the love and the many losses, and for the happiness of the moment. To tell the truth, I just need to cry for no reason I can think of.

31

THE PRESENT FINDS THE PAST

I t's all over, but really, it is just the beginning. After more than fifteen years, the shadows turned into my own flesh and blood. My parents, Frau Graf, Herr Rosen and I are sitting in Frau Graf's living room.

"Yes, we were running from the Russians that day," says Mutti, "along with thousands of others."

"You wore a light blue dress with bright red blood." She is amazed that I remember.

Vati keeps staring at me, wanting to talk, but he is overwhelmed.

"Give him time," says Mutti. "The dark side of life still casts its shadow over the light you brought." She makes music with her hands and poetry with her words. I am intrigued.

We decide that I will stay with Frau Graf to finish the school year while my very own Mother finishes her concert tour. Then I'll spent my two weeks of Easter vacation in Bonn and meet my older sister Ulrike. An older brother, Eberhard, lives in the

US. He has plans to visit in the summer. At that time, I will enroll at the University of Bonn. Maybe study law and work with Herr Rosen one day, catching the truly wicked.

It is late. Herr Rosen and I take my parents to the train station. It's a bittersweet goodbye. We barely met. But Mutti is right, it will give us time to absorb and adjust, and I need to decide what it is I want to do with my butcher shop.

Am I glad? I am numb is all. In the mornings, I wake up pinching myself to feel the joy. Then I get numb again. Letters begin to arrive from my parents, nearly every day. Then Ulrike and my brother Eberhard join the madness.

"Mother," I write, "I don't know them. They smother me with love. I'll explode."

"Don't worry," she writes back. "Your siblings have loved you all their life. Enjoy their letters, get to know them. No pressure to write back. Love is not a competition, and your other families are your family, too. Visit us as often, as long or as short as is right for you, my girl, my dearest dearest girl." I feel her rough hands softly touching my cheek and suddenly miss her, relieved that I don't need to belong the most to anybody.

Herr Rosen got in touch with the lady from England. His brother and wife died in a car crash. They left behind a little girl, Susanna, four years of age. Poor Herr Rosen. He lost his parents and older brothers, and now his favorite brother while I found a whole new family. I am truly sad for him.

But there is little time for grief. Frau Graf has finally agreed to marry Herr Rosen and we drink to it. Why did she wait so long? She wanted to find their daughter first. But now they will have a daughter. They will pick Susanna up over Easter and adopt her during the time I'll spend in Bonn. What's left is to find the meaning of it all. Isabel tells me not to look for a meaning. It will come on its own when it means something.

My fake Mother got a visit from her brother, an aunt and a cousin. Now they want to meet me. I don't think so.

"Maybe one day when I am wise enough to turn the bitterness towards her into some kind of better-ness," is what I write back, full of myself for such a clever sentence.

They reply that it's not for Mother's sake they ask. They met her for fifteen minutes, and that was ten minutes too long. They want to meet me for my sake. I sound so extraordinary from the little Mother talked about me!

Wait! What? What the hell would Mother say that was so flattering? I want to know. If it's good, I might consider visiting the old bitch one day, but don't count on it.

32

REBORN

Time is pulling me forward on the journey into my past. The train rattles and hisses, lulling me into a skittish sleep. A loud whistle jolts me awake and I decide to write letters, even though I just left.

Dear Frau Rittenmaier,

Without you, it would have been MY fly covered corpse hanging on a hook.

I love you and Herr Rittenmaier, I love the kids and I love your house. Remember, I thought you two looked alike, you and your house! Warm and welcoming. On second sight, you are softer, better proportioned, and you do not rattle when it is windy! See you soon,

Loving greetings from the bottom of my heart, Klara

Dear Frau Graf,

When we first met, you took my breath away. You are one of three amazing women that changed my life. You saved me from being raped. It was YOUR voice I heard "Bite hard, my girl, bite with courage!" Thank you!!

You and Herr Rosen mean the world to me. I can't wait to meet Susanna. We'll have a lot to talk about by then.

Klara with oodles of love

Dear Frau Dietrich, Herr Dietrich and Isabel and Nicholas,

Now I have my very own family. I am nervous to meet them all, but you helped show me the way with your love, patience and kindness. Herr Dietrich, your smile made me feel safe when times were tough.

Isabel, tell Harald I still love him but am glad that you got him. And Nicholas, your fingers are meant for the piano. Keep hitting those keys. See you soon again,

Much love to you, Klara

Then I write another short one to Frau Graf and Herr Rosen.

By the way, my dear ones, I heard that Bonn University Law School is crawling mostly with men. My goal is to seduce every one of them without getting pregnant. What do you think?

I know what you think, but a girl can dream, can't she?

Hope you are doing fine, especially you, Herr Rosen. Remember, no matter how difficult, Susanna needs happy parents!

Love again, Klara

. . .

I am in Bonn now, getting to know my big sister Ulrike who remembers me so well. All day long we fill in the blanks, but nothing serious or painful. Not yet. The closest Mutti comes to my past is to suggest I write down my story.

"It will help get rid of the demons you still carry. And one day, when you look back, you can write an awesome book."

Yes, I could. I like the thought.

There's a beauty in being so oddly connected, in recognizing my toes on Vati's feet, my nose in a grandmother's face. Ulrike and I, emotional over the silliest things, like staring into the mirror and seeing each other in each other. I used to be her doll. She'd stuff my mouth with unknown delicacies, and above all she loved me. She still does and follows me around afraid I might get stolen again.

Mutti's softness surrounds me all day long yet never too much. It's as if we never left each other's side. When we play the piano together, we are truly in tune. If you hear sour notes, maybe the piano needs tuning.

Then there was this morning in the bathroom with Vati. He had shaving cream over his face. We both stared at the mirror.

"Am I truly your daughter? It's still hard to believe. You are bowlegged, I am not."

He took his brush with the shaving cream, slapped it over my face, and simply said:

"Now we look alike." And we do, and we laughed, and slowly I am becoming his daughter.

Then comes the most memorable, meaningful evening of my life ever. It's after dinner, my time in Bonn nearly over. We are looking at old slides from when I was born to when I was stolen. Vati projects them against a wall. They are large like in the movies and so very real, and they ignite strong emotions. Deeply buried memories are welling up through layers and layers of muck. A photo with Mutti and me cheek to cheek makes me tremble and cry. I run to the wall, must touch these moments, these shadows, must rub and dig my fingers into them, not let them get away again. Now Ulrike is brushing my hair.

"You were two years old" says Mutti. On the next slide, Vati is reading a book to me, then my brother Eberhard is holding my hands for my first tentative steps. And the tiny white sweater with colorful cotton balls stitched across the front, I remember it.

Through these photos I feel their nourishing love seep into my skin. I am reborn into my family. I have found myself.

ABOUT THE AUTHOR

Beate Dayem Stamness lives with her husband in Petaluma, California, where they garden and play at being good grandparents.

www.ingramcontent.com/pod-product-compliance
Lightning Source LLC
Chambersburg PA
CBHW030119260626
47156CB00008B/2717